Praise for Sonia Taitz

"Sonia Taitz is an incisive, funny writer."—*People*

"Wise, witty, and often hilarious."—*Publisher's Weekly*

"Touching, sincere, endearingly besotted."—*Kirkus Reviews*

Praise for *In the King's Arms*

"Sonia Taitz's witty, sensuous prose enlivens this tale of two cultures converging in Oxford in the 1970s. Lily of the Lower East Side, daughter of Holocaust survivors, falls in love with a son of the English gentry and is drawn into his family drama. Taitz deftly contrasts the lovers' opposing worlds—and the surprising middle ground where they embrace."

—Barbara Klein Moss, author of *Little Edens*

"*In the King's Arms* is a deeply felt, lyrical novel, at once romantic and mournful, that brings to life the long tentacles of the Holocaust through the generations. In Lily Taub, Sonia Taitz has created an unforgettable, believable and sympathetic character—the young girl in all of us. The author's finely wrought observations about class structure in England, the vagaries of first love and the overriding possibility of redemption will stay with the reader long after finishing this book. "

—Emily Listfield, author of
Best Intentions and *Waiting to Surface*

"Who you are and where you come from are as indelible as the night, or in Lily Taub's case, the darkest night imaginable. Trying to outrun her world, headstrong Lily escapes to Oxford where she meets the gorgeous and aristocratic Julian Aiken—as English and Christian as she isn't.

Always playing in the background of their torrid romance is her parents' past. Her mother was raised in a concentration camp, and her father spent most of the war hiding beneath a barn in Poland, where overhead the "sweet cows" offered company and precious heat.

In her gloriously rendered novel, *In the King's Arms*, Sonia Taitz writes passionately and wisely about outsiders and what happens when worlds apart slam into each other."

—Betsy Carter, author of *The Puzzle King*

In the King's Arms

Also by Sonia Taitz

In the King's Arms

Sonia Taitz

McWitty Press   New York

This book is a work of fiction. The characters, incidents and dialogues are drawn from the author's imagination and are not to be construed as real. Any resemblance to actual events or persons, living or dead, is entirely coincidental.

Cover design by Jennifer Carrow
Interior designed by Abby Kagan

Library of Congress Cataloging-in-Publication Data
Taitz, Sonia
In the King's Arms: a novel / Sonia Taitz.—1st ed.
p.cm.
ISBN: 978-0-9755618-6-7

To Professor John Simopoulos,
genie of Oxford and fellow traveler

Love in its essence is spiritual fire.

EMANUEL SWEDENBORG

In the King's Arms

New York: 1975

HERE WAS A PLACE for everything, and everything was in its place but Lily. She had come to Europe in a great heat, pressing her attentions upon one of its most ancient institutions. To gain access to Oxford she'd had to get "A" after "A" every day of her schoolgirl life, then flag them at the Doorkeepers of Western Civilization. Years of sprawling across the desk with outflung arm, pleading to be "called on," annunciated by the teacher. And later, at college, her perfect papers: "well observed," "sensitive." Lily entertained the idea that she could amount to something spectacular. The Messiah, who had not yet arrived, could well be a woman, particularly in these times.

Her poor old father had shelled out the necessary cash; he was so proud of his girl. It was two against one, and the mother had lost. She pushed together a heap of crumbs on the table. "Boy-o-boy, you'll be some great lady," said the father, as his wife (Lily's mother) grumbled. He believed in providence, in "election," in spirits that are suddenly whisked from corked flasks to do marvelous things. This was because of what had happened to him, how his own life had been saved, thirty years ago, in Europe.

"Great lady," her mother finally said aloud, a sullen echo of her father's blessing. It wasn't jealousy. It wasn't that the Nazis had ruined her education. She thought Lily was running away from everything she knew. She thought Lily was running away from her.

Lily could see her point. They were sitting in their bright kitchen in the Lower East Side of New York City. Linoleum on the floor (a pick-up sticks motif in primary colors), tarnished pots and pans, daisy-patterned oilcloth, bird-drop on the sill. She looked at them and saw two elderly refugees. Modest, simple, straitened. Their shoulders seemed fragile under their clothes. They hadn't come from Oxford-Europe. They'd come from Eastern Europe. Although they didn't make the distinction; to them it was one bloody "old world," medieval checkerboard.

Her mother was tattooed: blue digits on her arm. Lily used to be ashamed of this, and this disloyalty shamed her too. Even at her Jewish summer camp she'd been sickened by shame, at a place where you'd suppose the other kids had parents like hers. They didn't: they had managed to find parents who played ball with them, who wore white sneakers and brought them bite-sized Snickers. Lily's grey-haired (what was left of it) father would grab a snooze on her hospital-cornered cot, the Yiddish newspaper shielding his face from the very brightness of a New World summer. Mother wore ankle socks and sandals; she offered soft, sad bananas, or hard-boiled eggs (wrapped in scrunchy tinfoil). She'd grasp the counselor's hand (her numbers went flying up and down, a blue whirl), and say "Senk you for vatchink mine Leely!"

They had raised their girl religiously: twelve solid years of yeshiva, to fortify her resistance to the outside world. Vassar College had been a frightening gamble, but it was in New York and reachable by car service. For years, Lily would not read the Bible in English; it seemed metallic, iced, pinched. Hebrew was dense and dark, like cello sounds, or chocolate. Melismatic melodies played in

Lily's head. They came from the synagogue up the hill; from below the fuzzy beard of the rabbi who first read her Isaiah's prophecies; from (as a child might say) thousands and thousands of years ago and far away.

At night she'd encounter anti-Semites in her shadowy bedroom, her parents' tormentors. She'd reason them away, talmudically deft, stabbing her finger into the air, listening to their responses as she stroked her chin. She managed to dissuade the English from kicking all their Jews out in the 13th century. She sat on the Pope's knee and tipped his skullcap to one side, so he looked like a merry-making Hassid. She converted the Spanish Inquisitors to the laws of *kashruth*: never again would they roast a Jew or eat paella. She made the Nazis cry: gosh, we're sorry! What in God's name came over us? The best part was forgiving everybody. "Oh, that's all right," she'd say aloud, magnanimously, "Just see that you behave from now on."

In a way, at twenty-one, Lily had grown deeply exhausted of the Jewish mania: a world consisting of Jews and non-Jews, the former radically monotheistic, ennobled by fires that cannot consume, messianic. And blessed with smarts. Her father had once said, "the dumbest Jew is smarter than the smartest goy." Of course, the goyim he couldn't forget were *muzhiks*: gap-toothed potato-heads with leering mugs. And her mother had a tendency to rattle off the following catechism: "Einstein Freud Marx Proust Mahler Mendelssohn Chagall and don't forget Dr. Jonas Salk, without whom they would all be cripples. And still they hate us!"

But in a way, and quite by nature, Lily was a Jewish maniac herself. The life she was living in America, relentlessly fair-minded, sane, secular, was, for her, mediocre. It offered no existential standoffs, no life-and-death crises. Even her parents seemed to soften and blur under equitable American skies. Lily was prime for zealotry.

She had none of their hard-won mildness. She had the memories only, without resolution.

People often wonder how those who went through what Mr. and Mrs. Taub went through could be so "well-adjusted." They were. Three decades after liberation, they casually alluded to the nightmare over crullers and coffee. Lily's mother sported jeweled bracelets on her numbered arm and wafted perfume from shoulders that brutal German men had beaten; she and her husband went out waltzing every Saturday night. It felt strange when Lily looked at her baby pictures, taken by her parents, knowing that their own pictures had been burned, that their parents themselves (her missing grandparents) had burned to anonymous ash and blown away. But they never thought of the pictures that way; they loved the pretty pictures. It was Lily who was blindly chasing ghosts.

Another thing about Oxford. The obvious: *Kultur*. God knows, Lily was a snob! She didn't hold with her father's smart-Jew-dumb-goy philosophy. Quite the contrary. The Anglo-Christian empire had sunk its stake into her imagination as soon as she read *Hamlet* (on a typical, schizoid yeshiva day in which she'd had Torah before lunch and Shakespeare directly after). She loved the romance of it; she loved the idea of times out of joint, of deaths avenged and unavenged. She had been conquered, too, by "Art History" with its painted crucifixes, and the image of the mother bereaved. She loved the strength of Renaissance brass, and the moody words "heath" and "moor." She curled up to regal, passionate Lord Byron. When he spoke of Asia, or George Eliot of Zion, or Blake of Jerusalem, their sudden intimacy made her shiver. Presumption inflamed her.

She sensed all along that what she wanted, in leaving the familiar, was not just abstract, but impossible. Lily wasn't going to recreate the fierce "Old World" anywhere. Oxford, in any case, while perhaps medieval, perhaps Victorian, was coolly removed from the passion of blood-hatred. She couldn't bring her past to it or it to her past. Even the little things she brought over to "brighten up" her room looked flat and small and lonesome there. Somehow the truth kept getting lost in the Atlantic Ocean, traveled either way. Lily might have believed in the impossible, but she couldn't hold both ends of it at once.

With one exception.

1

Europe, 1976

WHEN LILY FIRST SAW HER ancient college room, she felt doomed. It smelled of puke and mildew; a chipped sink gurgled dyspeptically in the corner. Her narrow bed was covered in what looked to be tartan burlap (not the generous, lumpy, duvet-smothered, stuffed-pony bed she'd envisioned). She saw a thousand wretched nights ahead, Oliver Twistian nights in which she'd go to sleep squirming and loveless and lost.

Down the hallway, doors were creaking and slamming. She could hear boisterous voices, English-accented (no: now she was the one with the accent), engaged in territorial frolics:

"Painsley! You sow! Want some coffee?"

"I'm ab-so-lyute-ly knackered!"

"MacAree's just down the hall."

"Where's the ruddy hammer, Pickles?"

She locked the door, sat down on her steamer trunk, and bawled. A minute later, her head picked up smartly as a key turned in the door. A sturdy West Indian woman strode in, dragging a vacuum cleaner.

"HALLO!" she boomed, looking directly into Lily's face. She wore a wide red headband and a blue housecoat. Her face was badly scarred, burned perhaps.

Lily wiped tears off her chin.

"I Hoover your dust balls," said the woman. "I Mrs. Dancer; yes. I wake up your lazy bones in the morning," she added, turning on the vacuum with a matter-of fact kick.

"YES!" she continued, bellowing over the wailing machine, "WHAT A DUST, WHAT A BIG DUST I FIND HERE, OH MY GOD . . . ." She ferociously pursued every inch of the room, and Lily sat, watching her. She envied her busy, purposeful life. She wondered how old Mrs. Dancer could be. Her calves were covered in coarse, pilled stockings, but her hands and feet were delicate and girlish.

Mrs. Dancer motioned Lily off her trunk, shoved it aside forcefully, and took care of the big dusty rectangle now exposed in the center of the room. "Yes," she said, kicking the machine off, at last. "Yes," scratching her nose with a long finger. "I knock up de lazy ones and make de bed tight like a drum." She noticed that Lily had been crying.

"I empty your bin." She swung Lily's trashcan up to her face, and peered inward. "Nothing in dere. You fill it up presently. You fill it wit your odds and ends, my dear." She gazed at the girl frankly, questioningly.

"Yes, I will," Lily conceded. She found herself having to cry again, at the assumption, hardly far-fetched, that she'd be living in this place for a good long time, and filling her bin up.

"You come from far away?" Mrs. Dancer stood at the window, leaning on a hip, pensively staring out into the world. From the frantic way she worked, one wouldn't anticipate the peaceful kindness she radiated at leisure. Lily stood next to her, shoulder to shoulder, looking out through the leaded windowpanes. A great, grey sky, heavy with moisture, dark with the tolling of bells. She pulled the window open and smelled the wet meadow grasses.

"Yes," she replied, "From New York City."

"You don't look English." A trace of approval.

Lily didn't know what to say to this. People were always puzzling over her looks. Her hair was light brown. (Some called it "dirty blonde.") Her eyes were green, like her mother's, and like her mother's, her nose was sprinkled with pale freckles.

"Almost Austrian," her mother would say ("almost"—Lily thought it sounded a bit like "dirty blonde"); "we could have smuggled you through." Probably not through England, in any case; Mrs. Dancer's evaluation was accurate. Lily's cheekbones were as wide as a Tatar's, her eyes sliced long, and few Anglo-Saxon women had breasts as round and full. In England, her lush hips seemed somewhat decadent, assailable.

"Where are you from?" she asked.

"Jamaica." She was still looking out the window. "I from Jamaica, Kingstown, you know." Up close, her eyes glistened, two precious stones in her ruined face. She sighed patiently. "What's the time, dear?" Lily told her. She turned and left, sliding her heavy vacuum behind her.

2

OXFORD CARESSED LILY'S SENSES in a bittersweet way. Church bells tolled from Gothic spires, summoning in her a nostalgia she couldn't trace. Inside, fair young men sang Evensong, weaving dusk into dusk, spinning her backward into history. Five hundred years ago, they might never have met. She was very near them now and they were very near her. She could hear them, see them fly by on their jingling bicycles, scarves streaming. Her feet matched theirs on the echoing cobblestones. They were gentle and young. A decent folk. Now that she'd traveled across time and the great Atlantic to see them, could they but be kind to her? She was thinking of "kindness," like an orphan.

If you asked Peter Aiken, he'd say that he rescued Lily from the worst possible fate at Oxford: association with the "wrong people." She was lonely, looking up at the crumbly yellow-brown stones, following the white ribbon trail of swans on the River Isis, shopping for cream-cakes in the covered market, sipping mulberry wine in an ancient tavern. It was all too scenic to enjoy. Peter discovered her in that ancient tavern, quite by accident. He'd taken some girl into the alleyway to kiss, while Lily'd been moodily strolling by, glass in hand, and literally bumped into them. The girl, Flora, she recognized from her college. She was one of those girls with the V-neck sweater and the neat row of pearls. But she didn't think she'd ever seen Peter before. He had a high forehead, a mixture of nobility and a tendency to baldness. What hair he had was beige as an Afghan hound's and hung entirely behind his head. He kept his neck and throat bare. An excellent choice: they were pure Modigliani. And he wore yellow kid gloves ("gantlets," he called them).

"I'm sorry," she said, as Peter wiped some wine off Flora's skirt. "You look familiar," she added loonishly to the girl. This was no time to strike up a conversation; Peter and Flora still retained a hot and bothered look from their necking; they did not seem in need of chums just then. They stared at Lily. Then Flora said, politely, "Oh, yes! I'm sure I've seen you in college."

What a kind soul, thought Lily. Then she noticed Peter's baleful expression.

"What's the matter?" she said.

"What do you mean by that?" he said.

"The way you're looking at me."

"Are you a student here?"

"Of course she is, darling," said Flora, soothingly.

"Well, what are you doing in this bloody tourist's pub?" he bellowed. "Where one is meant to find no one whom one knows! Where one is meant not to be spied on! Haven't you any sense at all? I tell you this for your own advancement!"

Lily burst out laughing. Peter had a ridiculous pink face. Then he laughed, too, a trifle reluctantly. He asked Lily if she was a "Yank." She admitted it. She said she was Austro-Hungarian "by blood," though, descended from impoverished royals, deposed but proud. Peter actually seemed to believe her. He nodded slowly, approvingly.

"Do you dye your hair that color?"

"Yes," said Lily. "I do. Its natural color is white like Andy Warhol's. We came over from Hungary together. He's albino. Mine's white by accident of fortune. The fright of my family's sudden departure to the New World turned it overnight. That, and saying goodbye to all the faithful servants."

"Do you like New York? Are you a millionairess?"

"Why do you ask?"

"I never ask. I demand. I demand to know. But I suddenly couldn't care less. You've got lovely Magyar cheekbones. Come here. What's this you're drinking? Fruit juice?" He stared at Lily's mulberry wine. "Never drink this vomit again!" Flora fidgeted restlessly.

"Now," he said, taking Lily's glass away and throwing it at the stone wall. "Would you like to have a Pimm's cup in my room?"

"O.K."

"Flora, if you're going to sulk like that, just go."

"It's nearly suppertime," said Flora. "I'm eating in Hall tonight. I had better go." She played with her scarf. "Will I see you in The Grapes later on?"

"You might," he said. "Don't eat brussels sprouts, just in case."

He walked off with Lily. His college was Christ Church, and his room extraordinarily studied. An antique mirror bearing poorly distinguishable comedy-and-tragedy masks hung on the wall over the bed. A sheepskin rug was tossed on the floor, and upon it a copy of *Les Fleurs du Mal* was exhibited, the moaning nudes writhing on the splayed cover. The wall across the bed was plastered with art postcards from around the world. Peter could identify them all, and liked to. He made Lily a Pimm's cup. She sat in an armchair that was draped with a ratty fur stole.

"So you're new," he said, draping his bones on the bed. "A fresher."

"Yes."

"I'm fourth year," he said, proudly. "Modern languages." Actually, Lily, pursuing a second degree, was no younger than Peter.

"Which ones?" she prompted.

"Italian and German. It's quite tough. Had to go to Munich last year."

"Didn't you like it?" Boy, she thought, her mind humming. Munich. Dachau's neighbor. And this new chum of mine was there, oh so casually.

"No. I loathed it. Fatheads. Boors. The girls had thickened calves. You've heard of 'the fatted calf,' haven't you? Those girls had two, each. Ankles like tree trunks. It's no wonder they lost the war. No pretties to die for. None that I saw, at any rate. None like you."

Lily was just thinking that she found him sexually repulsive, although otherwise quite genial.

"I spent my spring vac in Vienna," he continued. "Even worse, those women. Cows. Nasty, too. A ghastly, fin du siècle feeling. And everyone eats far too much. *Schlag. Schlag* on their coffee, *schlag* on everything, *schlag* on their *schlagged*-up arses."

"Did you know it means 'beaten'?"

"Of course I'd know, fish-face. Like 'whipped' cream or 'distressed' leather. Hmmm . . . What of it? Getting randy, are you now? Pimm's does that to girls."

"No!" she giggled. "It's just that my mother uses that word when she tells me a particular story about—"

"Yes, I'm sure I understand. About beating the servants in the Schloss. Poor Austro-Hungarian Royal. You must miss your waltzes now and then. *Mein Liebe . . .*"

"Well, not really," she said calmly. "You see, we're not all that homesick. You see—we're—we're Jewish. So we took the world tour on a flying boot kick. Mother survived the death camps. She uses the word '*schlag*' to illustrate a tale of being beaten on the head."

That shut him up. Peter's left eye twitched a hair's-breadth.

"My father hid underground in Poland," said Lily. "A Polish family told on him. They'd dug up the grave of his infant son, saw that the baby was circumcised, and found my father, not ten yards away, hiding under a barn. He went straight to Dachau. It's conveniently situated near Munich. Where you had such a bad time with your fatted calves. Small world," she concluded, with a thrill.

"What do you want me to do about all of *that*?" he said sharply. "It's you who's small. Dragging your wretched family into my anecdotes. I'm really rather impatient with 'tragedy' anyway, particularly when borrowed. Look at you, unscathed. What did you suffer?"

"Well, looking at all the corpses hanging on my family tree hasn't always been fun. I've lived in that world all my life. And they've always reminded me that I could have been born earlier, in Europe. You'd have watched me taken away."

"But you weren't born then. And neither was I."

"Anyway, you're not Jewish," she muttered, "and nothing truly shattering ever happens to inbred Aryans like you."

"What rot. We have our tragedies."

"Not mass ones."

"Oh, shut up, you envious, grudge-bearing witch."

"No, you shut up, you pretentious snot ball. I don't like you anymore."

"I don't like you either. What's your name, smiley?"

"Lily."

"Lily—quite a pretty name. I find this conversation tiresome. You take things too much for granted. I try not to. What are you reading?"

"Medieval English Literature."

"That's respectable. Learning to speak properly is always a challenge, not that I would know, as I was born articulate. Are you at all clever?"

"Clever enough to be here without centuries of family connections."

"Parvenu. I'm the cleverest one in my family."

He got up suddenly and put a record on the turntable.

"You'll like this," he said.

The singer screamed:

They call me Trevor!
I ain't half clever!
They call me rod!
But I'm a sod!
They call me Rick!
I'm good and thick-
-'Eaded!

"Don't like music?" Peter lay back on his bed, laughing. Lily's face was scrunched up amusingly, as though she'd sipped quinine. "Wait. There's a ballad coming up. You'll love the ballad."

The ballad went like this:

When I look into your face
Of all the human race
I see our petty pacing
To my bed, my friggin' bed!!

When I look into your eyes
Which futilely disguise
You're achin' to be taken

To my bed, that friggin' bed!!
But when I looked inside your ear
My dear, it seemed so drear
To think of pig-hogs cheerier than we. . . .

And when I looked between your lips
I saw them apple-pips
Which told me you'd had tips
From knowledge-tree!!

So darlin' look at me
I'm randy and you see
My pretty poetry can't last all night

Unbutton all them clothes
Rip off them panty-hose—

"Enough," said Lily.

"It's not over yet." Peter shot her a look that made her nervous.

"Peter, I'm leaving."

"All right, I'll turn it down."

"Off!"

He turned it off.

"You're really very pretty," he said. "Very tasty." He had one hand on his lips, sizing her up. She noticed that his fingernails were black.

"Peter, you have a girlfriend." And thank God for that, she thought.

"But Lily, I don't know what you could mean."

"Well, who was Flora, then, your niece?"

"Flora! She's just—she's not even a possibility. I've known Flora for ages. Centuries. I grew up with Flora. I played doctor with her. I have seen her prepubescent vagina. I saw it at five. I saw it at ten. I couldn't bear to see it again. God, it must be *huge* now."

"Well, you won't see mine now either," said Lily, defiant, laughing.

"Oh, hell!" he said, "I've seen a million twats."

"Besides, I don't believe a word you say. You don't make out in an alley with a childhood friend."

"I do!" He screeched. "And there's an end to it!"

He took down a straw hat from the cupboard and put it on his head. It was a Mexican hat, the sort with bobbling tassel-balls.

"My dad thinks I'm bent, anyway. Got this on your backwards continent. City called Acapulco. Shat all day, under this very hat."

"I don't think you're bent."

"Thanks, acorn."

"Crazed, yes, but not bent."

"You're darling."

They got to be good friends. The next morning, when Lily sat down for breakfast in her usual seat, amongst the dullest young people she'd ever known, Peter (who'd apparently spent the night with Flora) came to her rescue again. A thick-nosed Scot had turned his huge head to her, explaining some of the chemical and physical properties of eggs. His spectacles kept sliding down, and he kept patiently bringing them back up. Luckily, this gave Lily something upon which to fix her attention as she pretended to listen. He seemed to have a little crush on her.

"You take yourrr scrambled," he burred into her face. "Yourrr harrrd-cooked. Yourrr thrrrree-minute egg. It's all the same prrrinciple, lass!"

"Oh, is it?" she asked, trying to be pleasant.

The "Pseuds" (Peter's group), had they heard the exchange, would have laughed heartily. Their laughter was rich and unchained. Peter's arms were spanning the air like Nijinsky's. His long unbuttoned cuffs trailed theatrically behind the gesture, into his oatmeal. He caught Lily's eye, stared at her tablemates, and gestured, "Why them?" with a gorgeous grimace of sympathy. She excused herself and took her teacup over to Peter's table.

The conversations she heard there were hard-hearted, Nietzchean. They shocked and delighted her. Poets laureate and doddering dons got no pity. Everyone was laughable: the very poor, the very rich, the very clever, the very dim. Everything was ludicrous; everyone had a filthy little secret. What did Peter's tender yellow gloves conceal? Nicotine stains, those dirty nails, or the ink of his own secret poetic efforts? He never admitted being a dandy or a scribbler, but he smoked with an ivory holder between his dingy teeth, and hinted of folios.

Lily enjoyed these snide deductions. They were a relief from her own sympathies, which had sworn that the knowable world was worth knowing and good. It was a relief from the Judaic tyranny of logic, law and fairness.

The Pseuds seemed to like her. The best thing about her was her accent. New Yorkers were tough, like Jimmy Cagney. They said "gimme" and "yeah" and "gonna" and "gotta;" they could dance. As though Lily weren't milk-fed. As though she belonged to a gang that wore lead-lined berets and shouted at "cops." Michael, Peter's boy-Friday, was a lover of movies (he spoke of "the Coast" with a deep and innocent longing). He asked Lily about Lenny Bruce as though she had nodded in hazy dives for decades.

Peter observed her kiddingly bluff her way. He found her enormously sweet.

3

L
ILY CONTRACTED MONONUCLEOSIS during the second week
of term. (The English called it "glandular fever," as though
to comment on the unchecked, yearning humors of the
afflicted.) At first, it had offered an opportunity for understanding the strange new world at a distance. Nothing was demanded,
tutors sent good wishes, and Peter and his friends came bearing
gingerbread men and anemones. She slowly improved, rising into
the midst of enterprises she had never consciously begun. Where
was she? England? Were these her friends? Was she truly expected
to know anything about Alexandrine verse? Then, of necessity, she
adapted. These were her chums, these English kids, whose verses,
whose cultural history, she knew so much about. Sure.

Mononucleosis, or "glandular fever," struck Lily as largely a psy-
chogenic disease. It fed for a long time on her mind. Lily wondered at
herself when relapses recurred and recurred. Her body felt defeated
just when her mind seemed bent on doing well. Everyone advised her
to "breathe deeply," that fatigue would vanish if only one breathed
deeply, but each time Lily breathed deeply, she seemed to draw inside
herself a large filthy bag of vapors that weighed her down like ballast.

Mrs. Dancer brought her breakfast on the worst days. She
seemed to know when Lily was feeling wretched. She'd sit on the
edge of her bed and chat as Lily chewed.

"It's no wonder to me that you're poorly, Lee-lah," she'd say. (Lily liked this novel pronunciation of her name; it was like a pet name for her; only Mrs. Dancer had "discovered" it). "You been travelin' far. You be homesick now."

Lily was too tired to agree; she thought she might cry if she did. Looking into that open, kindly face (so unlike her mother's, so motherly) filled her with childish longings. That and eating lumpy porridge while wearing smelly flannels.

When Mrs. Dancer left her to clean other rooms, Lily would feel pinned to her bed, like a brooch in cotton. She could be found just lying there, mid-morning, half-asleep, suspended. On one such day, she jogged herself harshly and marched over to The King's Arms for lunch. That pub, she reasoned, could rouse the dead. The King's Arms was in fact a jolly, sprawling, lively pub. It was the epicenter of Oxford. Perhaps Peter would be there.

At first, she didn't see him. She ordered a half-pint of lager (disobeying doctor's orders) and sat down in one of the noisy smoky rooms, eavesdropping and making concentric rings on the wooden table with her glass. The weather was still warm, and people spilled out onto the street, like bubbles from a pipe.

She got up and took a walk herself, down Broad Street, stared up at the gargantuan stone noggins surrounding the Sheldonian, and enjoyed feeling tipsy and small and idiotic. As she turned to go back to the pub for a refill, she saw the most incredible looking Boy.

Incredible: black hair shining in lazy waves, throat covered by a faded, brick-red Indian cotton scarf, white shirt billowing, Hamlet-like, dissolving into soft, slate corduroy trousers. His jacket, voluminous and tweedy, trailed the heady smell of French tobacco. He noticed her, too: his eyed were brilliant, alert. A shade of blue. She followed him into The King's Arms, and stood near him inside, by the bar, transfixed as Titania. Oh Boy!

A Moorish ingénue begged him for one of "those delicious Gauloises," and he lit it for her. She told him her name: "Sabina." Lily wanted to rush up and tell him hers: "Lily."

"Sabina," he acknowledged distractedly, craning his lovely neck. Sabina looked at him through half-closed eyes, as though smoke had gotten into them. He asked her a question.

"Yes, a bit," she replied, silkily. Her head, tilted back. Appraising.

Sabina had a long brown body and thick dark hair to the waist, rough horse hair. Her eyes were amber-colored and slightly crossed, as though sexually dazed. An electric current razzled palpably through her limbs. Perhaps that was what made her hair so wild and her eyes split tracks.

"A bit?" he said. "What's that?"

"A bit," said Sabina, licking her lips as she thought, smiling, of a retort, "is what they put into the mouth of a horse so that he won't bolt, isn't it?"

Wow, thought Lily. Take that, you fine Boy.

He looked directly at Sabina. "Hmm," he said, "what are you, an Arab?"

"An Arabian stallion. Prize."

"La mare." He touched her horse hair.

"La fille."

"La filly?" He had his finger between her teeth.

"La filly mignon."

"I shall have you for dinner, then," he said.

Good God! They sat down at a nearby table, and Lily sat right by them, ears cocked.

"Oh, yes," she heard Sabina say. "I'm reading metallurgy. Ask me about alloys. Smelting. Welding. What college are you in, Julian?"

Julian. A lilting, faraway sound. The Boy was named "Julian." If she said the name, he'd turn his head.

"And what are you studying?" There was nothing arch in Sabina's voice now. That puzzled Lily. Now that they'd moved a bit in on each other, would she be all frank and open? That would bore him, doubtless. Metallurgy, of all things. Perhaps this Sabina-woman was a bit of a twerp. Lily took a seasoned look at her. No; she wasn't.

"Actually, I'm Ethiopian," she was saying. She was wonderfully mannered at moments, actressy; she seemed to accommodate Julian's hard gazes with an array of poses. In the way that a kneaded muscle yields luxuriously to the hand, in the way that a neck caressed curls vine-like, or a cat's stroked belly yearns its length across the floor, Sabina surrendered to Julian's eye with an exercise of parts beheld. He took in her hair: she hung her head sideways, and locks of the stuff dripped coolly on his arm (looking for a hairgrip she'd dropped, she said). He looked at her puff-lips: she placed a nut in her mouth, chewed it thoughtfully, licked salt off the tip of her thumb. Her waist (as she stood at the bar to get the next round) was long and sinuous; she leaned on one leg, then swung to the other, then back. A sort of hula. And when he stared at her eyes with his handsome eyes, hers widened, as though with pleasure or fear. She towered over him, holding their drinks, and then sidled over, sitting closer than before.

"*She's* been staring at me," said Julian abruptly, pointing to Lily. Lily spun her head away, burning with self-consciousness. Sabina turned around to see her. She burst out in peals of laughter. Very funny. She arched her head back so that her throat could be seen.

"Do you know her?" she asked. Julian didn't choose to answer for a drawn-out instant. Lily felt his eyes crawl all over her. They were absorbed, and insolent.

"Yes. She's my lover," he finally replied. "And Lord, what a dainty dish she is to set before a King."

Lily thought perhaps she'd better leave. And then Sabina stood up angrily.

"You're joking!" she said. "Aren't you?" Now there was a sad stupidity in her tone.

"Oh, goodness, no. I'm serious. I couldn't joke about a fuck like that. Be like denying the Godhead."

The words were arch, but his voice sounded sincere. Lily puzzled this for a moment. And then Sabina flew out of The King's Arms; she was passionately fast. A moment later, Julian left the pub. Lily imagined him chasing Sabina, eyes glued to her ass. She rolled it as she walked. He must have thought it was built for his pleasure. But then she turned the corner sharply, and Julian did not.

He stood still in the street, then returned to the pub. He sat down next to Lily. As he opened his mouth to speak, she felt woozy. She felt he might say anything, and she might listen to it. And just then, Peter entered into The King's Arms.

"*Mon semblable, mon frère!*" he roared happily.

"So that's where you've been!" To Lily, he said, "I see you've met my little brother. I hope he hasn't behaved naughtily."

"He . . . yes, he has," said Lily, after a moment. She looked at Peter with wonder, then regained her pace. "He's a flirt, a venereal flirt, and I was just about to tell him off."

"Oh, yes," said Peter. "Many's the time he's climbed Mons Veneris. Scaled the peaks, where the air's thin."

Julian laughed, avoiding Lily's eyes. She was having great difficulty avoiding his. Finally she rose, and said, "I've got an essay to write on the effect of the Middle Ages on the poetry of Coleridge. I'd better go."

"Which poem?" said Peter.

"Oh . . . 'Kubla Khan,' or 'A Vision in a Dream.'"

This struck her as funny even as she said it, and she began laughing helplessly. Julian laughed too, drowning her out, so that she nearly forgot the sound of her own laughter, or whether she'd been laughing at all.

Peter became a trifle crusty. "What's so bloody funny, you imbeciles?" They couldn't honestly say.

"Is it me?" he went on worriedly. "Is there something in my tooth? I've just had spinach and mushroom quiche."

Peter was quite endearing at times. Lily kissed him on the nose and left, thinking how strange it was that she'd put her mouth on the nose of the brother of the magnificent Boy. As soon as she was on the street she realized she might not see Julian again. She fought off this disturbing notion, raced back to college, and tossed off a killer essay on Coleridge and fantasy.

4

FEW WEEKS LATER, Peter invited Lily to a party given by
"OUDS," the Oxford University Dramatic Society. He
was showing off for her. This wasn't a mere gaggle of snot-
nosed intellects. This was the poseurs' very throne-room. Outlined
lips and eyes were *de rigeur* for either sex, as were boas of fur or
feather. Males were either slim-hipped serpents (nipping their iced
vodkas) or triple-chinned Falstaffs (swigging mead). Women, either
sepulchral ravens (with pointed, spasmodically gripped talons), or
lush vamps, teetering on spiked hoof.

Cocktails were chugged down with snorts and wheezes of self-
mocking pleasure. As though this were the roaring twenties, redux.
Yips and titters applauded the diverting names: "Sloe comfortable
screw?" Tee-hee!

"Pink Lady?" Hoorroar!! "Black Russian?" Ho! Ho! Marf!
Marf! These interpreters of the word knew how to applaud an apt
one. What these drinks actually tasted like could hardly concern
those who on the stage took water for wine. The fancy of the names
themselves was theatre to them. Indeed, it seemed to Lily that many
had been dubbed at birth to thespian knighthood with names that
would read well on the program: Roland, Cordelia, Ivor, Cressida,
Tristan, Rupert, Maeve.

Peter ignored Lily from the moment they arrived. He was captivated by this scene, to which he had not fully been admitted. He was still, to be blunt, small beans. His first attempts at acting had not all been successful. He was recalcitrant until he saw that he was appreciated, but he was not immediately appreciated, because of his recalcitrance. He had some native talent, though, which shone through everything he did, from the moment he received the script, brushed his straying hairs from his face, and stared silently into the eyes of his auditioners, to the moment his voice attacked the air. The only problem was that this confidence did not last. He could make the lines scan, but the emotions he was called upon to produce seemed to hang back within him.

Dogged effort had led him to small parts, in which he'd gained reassurance. He was a spear-carrier (literally), a delivery boy, scenery (the setting sun, a stone wall), a corpse, that sort of thing. He got used to the stage, he went out to the pub with the Rolands and the Cordelias, and he effortlessly began remembering the plum roles by hearing them repeated, unchangingly, night after night. He smelled the musty costumes and listened to the jungle din of spectators' giggles and coughs and big roars. There he was, bellowing "WAR!!" when the placid old world thought it was at peace. There he was, delivering the crucial missive to the King, an insolent grin on his lips like the subject sensing the King's mortality, like a bit-player on the rise sensing the star's mediocrity.

Soon he hungered for greater parts. Meaty ones. He was often summoned to second auditions now, but inevitably he ended up with conciliatory bit parts. One problem he had was fluency with accents. There was only one kind of speech that Peter was master of: English, Upper Class. He could not spit out a syllable of Cockney, Scouse or Geordie, let alone dialects more obscure. For this reason he'd recently lost a role in a play he adored, *Look Back in Anger*.

"Don't sound angry enough to me, lad," said the director, patting him on the shoulder as he grabbed back the script. Still, there were many good parts available for his Oxbridge tones. It was just a matter of making the right connections and not losing heart.

Shelagh Eveline Fanning was there, just as he'd hoped. She was famous, an English tutor at Wadham, with amazing connections to the theatre. Behind-the-scenes connections: she knew everyone by nickname, by proclivity. She was like the Mother of them all: huge, massive, laughing. Her largeness lay not so much in her flesh as in her bones; she seemed hewn from stone, a Maillol. Her feet, though, were tiny and delicate; she took little steps to the right and to the left as she spoke, giving true meaning to the word "patter," belying the sonorous sounds she produced from her enormous chest. She wore a heavy, leaf-green cape. She was surrounded. Peter edged near.

Lily saw Peter nodding his head slowly, eyes planted loyally on Fanning's moving mouth. Fanning seemed unaware of him. She began to declaim. A hush fell over the room.

"Acting," she said, "acting!"

Lily started to giggle, and everyone shot her such dirty looks that she left the room and sat in the bathroom for a while (on a toilet with the lid down). Ever since she'd met Julian, she was slightly short on control.

"Acting," repeated Fanning, once more. "It is nothing but release. You are tight-faced, you English."

Fanning was of course Irish. "You *need* to be released. But acting is quintessentially English as well. A paradox. An extreme, wedded to its opposite.

"For acting," she continued, "is your tradition. Old and rich. You British actors" (they thrilled to be called "you British actors") "share a cozy, familial kinship. You're very clubby. Well and good.

"It is lunatic, it is wild, but acting is bounded and controlled, a means of insulation. *Coitus interruptus.* It tames and domesticates the furies. Mad, mad as an Irishwoman whose drink has not been refreshed—yes, that's better, thank you—but never exceeding the bounds of time and space. All fights end to applause—we hope. Empires carted off by curtain fall. Avowals of undying love, confessions of faith—all limited, all lies! All eternal TRUTHS!!!!"

Lily came back to hear these last words and fell victim to giggling again. Sabina, as it happened, was just behind her, and gave her a sharp smack on the back of her head. Lily turned around, and Sabina quickly said, "Oh, I'm sorry, I thought you were someone else."

Sure, thought Lily. And you are Marie of Rumania. She suddenly realized that Julian might be there, too, by some miracle of free association. But he wasn't.

The evening went very quickly just the same. Lily forgave Peter for ignoring her. She was even happy, towards the end, to see Shelagh Eveline Fanning accept her millionth drink from Peter's hand.

5

B Y SIXTH WEEK (each term had eight), Lily began to worry about the Christmas "vac." Term would end. Everyone would travel home to gurgling kettle, warm faded downy, and Christmas stocking stuffed with tangerines. Tangerines had already become available in Hall, a luxurious alternative to the perennial dull orange and dented apple. Tangerines; perhaps the name implied they came from Tangiers? She'd never thought about it before, but now she noticed the distances all things travelled to be in stately Britain. Portugal lent its port, and Jerez, its cream of Sherries. Pass the Madeira, Quentin, there's a dear. And everyone smoked imported cigarettes: Italian, Russian, French (oh, Julian!). Summoned with a careless match-flick, and a shallow suck.

Tangerines. The one on Lily's tray rolled languidly over on its side, revealing a voluptuous dimple. They called raisins "sultanas" here. A thousand and one sensual nights, dancing for the Sultan. Lily's room had been transformed in recent weeks. Wild bunches of anemones sprouted, dilated in fields of red and mad purple, whirling on furry axes, reeling into blackness. She lit dozens of candles every night, and watched them wildly climb the wall with flame-shadows. Dizzy songbirds spun round and round on her stereo's glinting stick, pierced through their core, cascading in sobs. Piaf, Holiday, Garland.... The world rolled in their throated hearts, poured forth in sultry threnody:

33

As far as I can see, this is . . .
Heaven
And speaking jus' for me
It's yoursss to share
Perhaps the glow
Of love may grow
With every passing day . . .
Or
We may never meet again
But then
It's not for meee to say . . .

Fragrant smoke rose, spiraling, like wails from minarets. She was dreaming, delirious. She saw herself breathing into the Boy's open mouth, their limbs entwined like wet, tropical vines. Who cared whose lips were whose, whose heart, whose dank tangled hair?

Often she awoke to the sounds of sheets of rain, dreaming of boiling tea, of tossing on an erotic sea, drunken and deluged, with the Boy.

Some nights, to anesthetize herself, she went into the Common Room and stared at the T.V. for hours and hours. In the Common Room, a muttonhead could sit undisturbed yet un-alone, until midnight, flanked by his fellows, drinking tea with a square of dusty chocolate. There, jolly images flashed on the screen like party streamers, providing the gracious excuse for warm bodies to clump together.

On this particular night, only two or three people were actually watching the program. That was enough, though. Lily pulled up an armchair, then went to make herself a cup of tea. She saw a copy of *Punch* lying on the counter and flipped through it as the water heated to a boil. She didn't get most of the jokes. She made her tea, bought a "Fiesta" bar from the vending machine, and sat down, smoothing her skirt.

Lily enjoyed the institutional clatter of the cup and saucer on her knees. Her chocolate had to last, so she played with it, sucking it, letting it melt on her tongue and slide down with the soothing tea. Once in a while, something jostled her funny bone. Then she squalled with laughter, slapping her knee: HAR! HAR! HAR! Like a seasoned bawd at the fair.

Was she going nuts? Another chockie lozenge and another cuppa tea. A-HAH HAH! A-HAH HAH! A slap and a slap! Then a program came on that really drew her in. It was about a Catholic girl, Geraldine, and her Jewish boyfriend, Samuel (according to English telly, all Jews had solemn Biblical names), and they were in love, and about to be hitched, but everyone thought the notion quite shocking. The Rabbi was paler than usual; the Priest, redder. So they decided to get together to hatch a scheme.

New Problem: the Priest's Cook didn't know what Rabbis ate.

"What shall I feed dear Brother Abraham?" Cook asked the Priest.

He replied in his funny, crusty way.

"Well, let me see, I'm giving it some thought, um—" said the Priest, scratching nervously under his clerical collar. He acted sort of the way old bachelors do on television when they have to diaper a baby. "No pigs, of course, or—"pause—"horses, camels, marmosets, corgis or yaks!"

Big guffaws.

"Do they eat fish," asked Cook, "of a Friday?"

The Priest knowingly replied, "Only if it's got fins and scales." The laugh track roared like the mobs on Bastille Day. But it was true, thought Lily. It was in Deuteronomy. *"Snapir v'Kaskeset."* What was so funny? Was God funny? She wanted to laugh, too (as teachers used to say when kids passed notes, snickering: "Kindly share your joke").

Sam and Gerry got married after all. Love conquers Religion; simple, snap, all solved in under thirty minutes.

It was about a quarter to eleven. Late enough to think of bedtime. Lily retreated into her room, stored her tangerine deep in the toe of a sweat sock, and hung it over the electric fire. Sanctuary, tangerine. She felt overwrought and lonely.

A loud rap on the door shook her up.

"Let me in, moo-cow!"

She pulled open the door and watched Peter sail into her armchair. He was too tall for it and sprawled, marking time with a heel.

"Be nice to me," he said, charmingly, and demanded a drink. They settled down to listen to Mahler together (he had bought her the tape). The music made Lily realize how sad she sometimes felt. Some deep potential in the changing chords made her feel abandoned. They marched inexorably, like strong and handsome troops, doomed to a fate that made her own seem thin and trivial. Being left behind, the ebb tide of noble causes.

Peter stirred in the chair. She suddenly found him intrusive, annoying. Was he going to react to the music by saying, "Oh, capital!" and flapping his bony hands? She raised the volume possessively, as though to anticipate drowning him out. He asked for more whisky and she swung the whole bottle at him. A late fall gustiness rattled her windows and made willows sigh large arcs behind Peter's head. This is homesickness, she thought. Whither thou goest, I shall go. Is anyone going anywhere that I can go? There was Peter, jabbering in a strange tone of voice. He was so pink and beaky; she could hardly take in a word he said when her ears felt so tight from the tears in her throat. Pink, pink, pink, like a baby put outdoors, screaming silently into the night. That was how she felt sometimes—her real heart, unheard in the din of her parents' pain.

"Hey, Miss!" she suddenly heard him say.

He gave her a huge pinch on the arm.

"What?"

"Don't you answer questions anymore? You look insane, by the way."

"You've made me black and bloody blue, Peter, you moron."

"Well, then, answer me."

"I didn't hear you."

"Deaf. I said, what are you doing over the Christmas vac?"

She turned the volume down. "Oh. I dunno."

"Look," said Peter quietly. "You simply can't stay here. If that's what you're planning. You'll be the only one around, and you're not even fully well."

"Yeah, I guess you're right."

"So I would like it very much if you'd impose on my ancestral home."

"You would?"

"Grace it with your unique form of barbarity."

"REALLY??" She was surprised to feel such deep relief. "Are you sure? Do you mean it? You've thought about it? You want me to come?" Lily did not give Peter the chance to respond. She grabbed his thin arm and danced him around the room at top speed; they made an exhausted, sloppy finish on the floor. God: Peter prickled with snideness, but really he was as softhearted as a moon cactus. He was smiling a smile that the upper class rarely achieves: his eyebrows had flown up, and his face looked naked and unusual.

Just then, she thought about Julian. He'd be there. She'd be in his home. The blood rushed from her head with one massive heartbeat. And Peter, amazingly, was saying, "The only problem will be my brother, whom you'll doubtless try to seduce. Don't. He is my mother's son. She feels he should be opened like a rose; doesn't seem to realize he's been pollinating for years. She won't appreciate it if you slaver on her Princeling."

"Oh, don't you worry," said Lily, choking on her own saliva.

"And you'll have to fit in," he said gruffly. "We don't coddle Yanks." He sat down and folded his fingers. "Mum's quite horsey. Kerchief tied under the chin, Wellies, walking stick, you know what I'm talking about."

"Oh, sure, I've seen television programs about the Queen." She paused. "Listen, Peter. Why is it that I don't see your brother in Oxford? Why was he in The King's Arms that one time, but never again?"

"Lily. Lily. You must be more discreet. You are making a lewd display of your vulgar, or should I say *vulvar*, thoughts. I won't have it. But since you ask, I am glad to tell you that Julian is not a student at Oxford, because, because . . . well, shall I say that one of us is tall, dark and handsome, perhaps, but one of us is not very clever? Julian may visit sometimes, but is not 'in' as you and I are."

"Oh, I see." This information failed to diminish Julian. Her own hyper-intellectual studies sometimes bored her stupid.

"Too bad you won't meet our real Dad. Julian looks just like him. Mum's remarried to a fat old accountant, with high scruples or something like that. He is a total prig. A few years ago, the two of them banded together and produced a round-headed, bald little half-brother—half-breed, I prefer to say—for Julian and for me. By now the little tyke smells just like dull, fusty step-dad looks.

They are inseparable. They listen to *Peter and the Wolf* together; they both know every fucking word. Archibald's a music snob. Knows all the *Köchel* numbers. He's criminally boring. Uses maps and dusty almanacs to answer questions, like that. Collects butterflies."

"Tell me about your 'real' father."

"Oh," Peter sighed, and was silent for a moment.

"He's wonderful, really. He gambles, he travels. He's naughty."

"So he's the fop you take after," Lily teased.

"What do you mean?" Peter snapped. "I don't have to take after bloody anyone."

"Well, do you look like him?" Another mistake. She saw that Peter was deeply unhappy about his looks.

"I told you Julian looks like him, didn't I? And I don't look like Julian, now, do I?" He paused, and sighed again. "No. He has dark hair and a smashing black moustache. Tremendous teeth, bright white, and thick eyelashes. Dad's a stew-eater, a heavy drinker, a creature of excess. You heard what Shelagh Eveline Fanning said about taming the furies, didn't you?"

"I must have been out of the room."

"Well. Artists do it. *He* can. He was an incredible actor at Oxford. He knew Shelagh Eveline Fanning when she was merely Shelagh Nobody. They ran neck and neck, if you know what I mean. He runs an acting school in Cannes now. Screws all the girls. They consider it an honor. It is."

"I'm very fond of dark men." This was the way to talk to Peter, as though people came in flavors. Bittersweet chocolate treats.

"You are, are you? Very typical. Even Mum was seduced, and she's frigid, you know. She had to divorce Dad; he was having his way with her too often. Smearing her lipstick. And he hated her horses, you know. Hated all the shitty paraphernalia. What my Dad loves, really adores," Peter's face seemed to imitate a more predatory relish than his own, "is seediness, tiptoeing into the boudoir, chuck under the chin, stolen kisses followed by savage fucks, that sort of thing. He's a do-it-your-selfer, a trellis-climber. You should see him in Hyde Park, wrapped in a blanket, eyeing the girls with that hard stare of his. They eye him too . . . ."

The hand that had been playing with his hair was now still, lost in a tangle.

"I look like Mum," he continued. "She's the one with no visible eyelashes, like a pig. But it looks right on her; she looks like someone singed them off, martyring her. And the weariest expressions: 'How you bruise me, Peter. How you wound me, Julian.' Like that. I suppose that's what attracted the pious Archibald to her, although what attracted her to Archibald I cannot say."

"Maybe she was tired of Hyde Park and mustaches. Maybe she wanted a real home, be it ever so homely." Lily sometimes, not often, thought this way.

"Homely is what she got, Lily. Archibald is sadly Dad's opposite. Convex belly to concave. Poor little Timothy will never know what it is to be madly in love with his sire. Little does he know that *Peter and the Wolf* is just the beginning of his burgher's existence. Now he's apparently imitating a piccolo all day. Then his voice will change, and he'll be an old bassoon like Archibald, pasting labels on his record collection. Clearing his throat when he has nothing to say. Wiping his glasses whenever he disagrees with anyone. They both make me truly sick."

"Timothy can't be blamed, Peter. I mean, he's just a little boy!"

"You're such a dope. I, for one, do not find the qualities of fetal life to be inherently endearing."

"Peter?"

"Yes, fish-face?"

You don't really hate your little brother, do you? You're lucky to have a little brother! I only wish I had any brother at all. It really does seem kind of medieval—"

"Try byzantine. Byzantine's the big word, lately."

"—to hate your little brother, and call him a 'half-breed'—"

"Well, sometimes, I call him 'The Usurper,' actually. Now, Julian and I will have to split our estate three ways."

"Oh, be quiet."

"Now, would you like to hear about the birth of this innocent child?"

"O.K."

"I'll tell you all about it, and you'd better not repeat a word I say. When Mum had Timothy, she had a difficult time of it. She was in hospital for a long time afterward. They thought she'd die, you see, delivering him. He's big and fat, you see, like Archibald. And she's frail."

Peter's gaze hung for a moment out of the window, in the direction of the willows that they could hear but not see, as though searching for diversion in the world beyond his thoughts.

"One of the doctors knocked out some front teeth, jamming in a tube to save her. She was still puffy and yellow when we finally saw her, Archibald, Julian and I.

"Do you know what Archibald said to my mother then?"

"Oh, Peter, I'm sure—" His chin was wobbling.

"Archibald said—Archibald said—'Helena, I can hardly believe that I married you, the way you are looking today.' For a minute, we all just waited for Mum to say something. She had closed her eyes in the middle of his sentence. I thought it might be the medicine, or the exhaustion, but then all of a sudden she opened them up, wide, and cried out: 'Oh, please! Archibald! Please!'

"He calmly said that he'd overlook her failings, as she'd delivered a son and heir, the pompous ass, 'an heir.' And she took his greasy, swollen fingers and kissed them gratefully. She looked up at him, helpless, with a sincere gratitude. She knows that her feelings for him will never change: she never loved him, and never will; she just needs him and was relieved that he wouldn't start veering off course, the way Dad did. Any movement away would have crushed her. She wanted to know that things would stay put. That she could stay put."

After a few minutes, Peter decided that he was starving, so Lily retrieved her tangerine from her sock, much to his tired amusement. She sectioned it, arranging it nicely on a plate with some plain chocolate biscuits. Peter rallied, commenting that orange and brown went together smartly, "Which is funny, you know, fish-face, because brown is so moo-cow tame, and orange, as the great Huysmans says, unnerves the jaded senses." Lily said that she couldn't agree more, and helped Peter dispose of the strange combination.

6

LATER, JUST BEFORE SHE FELL ASLEEP, Lily thought: what was wrong with the old bachelor finally marrying, finally loving his own son? He was going out on a limb for that boy, a fat old man becoming ridiculous. Exactly what was wrong with that? Was this soft spot undermined by his cruelty to his wife on the night of the birth, or did the cruelty make the soft spot miraculous?

Peter could be very biting, but tonight he'd been the kindest person on earth; he had invited her home with him. He'd recognized her loneliness, and her need. Some tyrants, even the worst, had loved animals. Didn't that spell out lost possibilities? Didn't that offer hope to know that these "almosts" exist? Not everything is ironic. Some contrasts spell magic.

Perhaps Peter had been exaggerating about Archibald. Perhaps Archibald had simply said that Helena didn't look well, had said it only out of real concern. Poor Archibald: a wife with a child at last for him. Marriage was probably the most exotic, horrifying venture he'd ever embarked upon. No wonder he liked to bury his kisses deep in the folds of his baby's soft neck, where they could at long last stay put.

7

THE GLOUCESTERSHIRE COUNTRYSIDE, where the Kendalls had their estate (inherited on Helena's aristocratic side), was blustery and cold in the wintertime. Lily's room was by far the frostiest she'd ever slept in: her muscles ached horribly each morning from tensing them rigid at night. At breakfast, Lily would try to smile cheerfully at her hosts, but found her face too stiff to widen; she displayed a few front teeth, like a cartoon woodchuck. She was stunned by their notion of how modestly living should afford comfort. Peter was quite tickled by her attempts to adapt to this Iceland.

"God, you poor thing, you're shaking," he'd say, barely suppressing a grin. He thought Lily was a spoiled American, and that this paradoxically frugal upper-class life was doing her "a world of good."

"Whatever doesn't kill me makes me strong," she'd respond sarcastically. Peter used to pat Lily's cheeks with brazen chumminess to warm her up. Lily swore that if he thwacked her face like that just one more time, she'd twist his beak off. After three or four days of this ritual she began returning some hearty slaps. They made a sweet vaudevillian tableau: four hands flailing, eyes glittering with concentrated play.

One morning, she greeted Peter with the first blow, a swift, wide-swinging one which deposited a crimson fireball on his pale, astonished face. His mother walked in just then. Peter regained his composure in an instant. His mother stared calmly at his blazing cheek.

"Lily," said Peter smoothly, after his mother had sat down to her food, "freezes at night." Helena Kendall, saying nothing, swung at her egg with a spoon. That night, Lily discovered an electric blanket under her meager duvet.

Actually, Helena and Archibald were used to the slapping business. Peter told Lily that he and Julian often scuffled, even bit each other, holding on with doggish tenacity, and bellowing muffled execrations as they gave and got. Julian was not there yet. He was visiting his father in France for a few days. Lily was a trifle relieved: she could not have taken everything in all at once.

The land around the Kendall home was green, good for grazing. The sky was low and wide, a lazy sky. Long rambles were an English tradition, and they were the tradition of this family as well. Lily, accustomed to subway trains ejecting her at designated intervals, was discomfited by natural obstacles. The countryside had no "stops;" entrances (into vast strange fields) and exits (from bramble bushes) were a matter of native strength and agility. She was a hopeless climber, and had trouble leaping across the narrowest of ditches. One time her jeans got caught on a gate that she knew was going to be nothing but trouble. It was high; the lock was tied with a complicated bit of hemp; there was an unconcerned but lethal bit of metal jutting out on top. The whole family swung gaily over, even the portly Archibald, who whooshed like a medicine ball as Lily stood lamely by, growing smaller and smaller as they all trekked on. She tried, but was impeded by the obligatory, oversized gumboots which she'd borrowed from the family arsenal; she ended up dangling by her seat. Peter looked backwards and nudged Archibald in the ribs. They laughed similarly: haw! Haw!

Haw! Lily ruefully considered: I thought Peter hated his step-father, but they make quite a good couple now. Laurel and Hardy.

Peter ran over to Lily and tore her down. Once back on her feet, she tramped hotly ahead, feeling their eyes upon her ragged end.

The sheep distracted her from her peevishness. They were really something to see. Dotting the hills with their lumpen presence. They were still, more still than the faint breezes that did not stir their thick wool. The wool seemed to fill the air with an off-white humming monotony. The sheep had other powers. You could not win a staring contest with these sheep. They were as unflappable as Kafka's extras, witnesses who had always been around, who had always understood nothing. They seemed painted into the landscape, an emblematic pattern.

In time, Lily became accustomed to the inhospitable outdoors, and did not mind so much being cold and wet and tired at once. Being outside in the country in winter was like heavy physical exercise. You sensed the nobility of the body's struggle, how it, like the mind and the soul, aimed for the infinite, for the "just once more!" It enjoyed its own strainings, tumbling from them into gratifying fatigue. Earned fatigue was the noblest thing in life, she thought.

After the walks, she felt a grand sort of solitude. She'd sit on stile, resting, as her heart slowed and silenced the rough banging in her chest. She'd feel that nature had had her, hard, like an ardent lover. Peter might sit next to her, breathing softly and radiating a surprising tenderness.

Archibald would hoist his little Timothy over the low, cracked bough of the yew tree just outside the house. His voice would travel faintly back to Lily, a note lower than the wind's; she'd hear him singing "Rock-a-Bye-Baby." She'd hear, but partly through her own imagination, the familiar words "when the bough breaks, the cradle will fall." Archibald's voice would fade in and out, carried toward her or away by the winds.

Mrs. Kendall might be staring at a riderless horse in the distance. The horse, tossing its mane, in the air gallivanting with the freedom of choice, freeing himself every which way and then, suddenly, magically, vanishing. Mrs. Kendall might say something like, "Tame a horse like that and you've got yourself a true-blue thoroughbred. Leave it wild, and you've got the very devil."

They'd turn to the shed, tug off their muddy Wellington boots, leave them behind, and enter the home again. Now it felt warm and clean. They'd sit down to a peaceful supper. Archibald would light the candles.

Lily was moved by it all, limp with happiness. Everything was rich, proffered and bountiful. Her eyes travelled from face to face. Archibald. Helena. Timothy. Peter. Peter was talking.

"Any word from the Princeling?"

"Oh," laughed Mrs. Kendall prettily. "You know Julian."

She said the name caressingly, and a demure hand fluttered to a slender throat.

"Yes, I have had that privilege," said Peter.

"I only pray," continued Helena, "that he doesn't end up suddenly straggling in on Boxing Day."

"What's that?" Lily's thin voice. She'd never heard of Boxing Day (to her it sounded, of course, pugilistic). Ordinarily, she wouldn't have asked; she'd have played along. Boxing? Boxing. But talk of Julian had loosened her lips.

"Well, my dear," said Archibald, "of course it's the day after

Christmas. Has a bit to do with putting sweeties in boxes, doesn't it," he added rhetorically.

Oh, like Purim, she thought. Purim was her favorite holiday. It featured Esther, a fantastic Jewish heroine (and beauty) who'd won the heart of a King. On Purim, one sent boxes of goodies around to one's friends, and to the poor.

"Archibald," Peter said patiently, "Lily doesn't celebrate Christmas, so how would she know that?"

"No, it's not that," said Lily hastily. "Nobody does 'Boxing Day' in America."

"Oh," said Archibald. "Oh, I see. How very strange." He was trying to coax a brussels sprout into Timothy's mouth. "How very strange."

"Stwange!!" said Timothy sternly. "Vewy stwange!"

Archibald wiped the baby's chin and cleared his throat. "At any rate, young Julian, harumm!! If he should happen to miss Christmas Day, Helena, I do not think it advisable to give him his present. One should not reward a show of disrespect."

"No pwezzy!!" Timothy kicked his legs gleefully under the table. "Naughty boy!" Quite a sturdy kid, thought Lily, feeling the blows under her vibrating plate. The accountant laid his hand firmly across the child's ankles. "Let his father get him a present out there in France, if he can't abide by the rules of place and time."

"Oh, darling, he'll surely be here," said his wife. "He's getting to be quite a grown-up and responsible young man. I shouldn't think he'd want to miss Christmas with his brothers."

"Well," grumbled Archibald, "he certainly won't have a proper Christmas out there. Do the Holy Romans have a Boxing Day, I wonder? I rather doubt it."

"At any rate, he'll be here soon," said Helena, ignoring this tirade against the Catholics. "All tall and straight and handsome."

"Handsome is as handsome does, Helena, as you know."

"Yes, dear. Yes, you're quite right." She stared distractedly at the pretty young girl Peter had invited. "He does begin to take after his father in certain distressing ways," she added quietly, as though to herself.

"I haven't told him that I've brought the Beauty home," said Peter, reading his mother's mind.

"Would you like some more lamb, dear?" Mrs. Kendall asked Lily. "There's quite a lot left, and it's especially tender.

8

WHISK, THE FAMILY CAT, was a survivor. As soon as he discovered that the guest's bed stayed warm from the electric blanket, he began to make a habit of spending his long, lazy afternoons in unheard-of comfort. Each evening, Lily would find him sighing contentedly in the deep rhythms of a good sleep. His soft white fur glowed from the country moon outside the window. Each evening, Whisk reluctantly awoke, yielding to Lily with a dignity that shamed her. She felt uneasy for several minutes after the cat padded, tail aloft, into the cold shadowy stairway, as though he had witnessed enough of her chronic selfishness. By the time Lily came shivering downstairs for breakfast, Whisk would already be lapping the "top of the milk" from a Beatrix Potter bowl. The bowl said: "Peter sat down to rest. He was very damp with sitting in that can."

Once, she touched Whisk's fur as he lapped industriously away. It was freezing, a fact that Whisk communicated nonchalantly, without having to look at her. He continued to nourish himself, offering no sign of acknowledgment. Lily stroked Whisk until, finally, a slow warmth began to rise, to respond, from the pink flesh below his fur.

Timothy, rubbing his eyes sleepily, wandered in. He stopped short, planted himself, and said: "Whisk is my cat," in a small voice that had no argument in it. He was stating a fact. His face, lunar in its roundness, completely filled Lily's field of vision. She was crouching at Whisk's side. She stared into the three-year-old's enormous eyes, which seemed, at that range, to waver into a single ocular glow. He was terrifyingly simple and right.

Peter said something mollifying, but whatever it was, it escaped Timothy, who kept glaring at the girl. She thought she noticed a puckering in his chin, the beginnings of a wobble in his chubby lower lip. It amazed her that she could not read the child's face well enough to say whether or not he would actually start to cry. Lily unfolded her body to the full, adult height, relinquished her claim on his animal, and gazed down at the top of Timothy's soft yellow hair.

"My cat," he repeated, down below.

Of course. Yours. Not mine, thought Lily. Your house, too. Your country. Your world. What native authority. She did not really like this creepy kid. How well he had adapted to the given. And so much had been given. An endless vocabulary of placement. Timothy was a piccolo, was he? One day a bassoon? A very orchestra to nestle into, conducted by a sceptered hand.

"Which *Peter and the Wolf* instrument am I, then?" she suddenly asked Peter. If you had to ask, you really didn't play. But Peter had an answer on hand:

"A jew's harp?" Eyes alive with presumption.

Being Peter, he meant no harm. Lily laughed cooperatively. Even Timothy caught the mood and shook from belly up like an old man, laughing, and Whisk rolled onto his back and stretched his legs majestically.

9

ARCHIBALD PLAYED THE PATERFAMILIAS with a pure concentration. It was easy to see that he'd come upon love in middle age; he expected perfect loyalty. This he received from Timothy, who was as reliable as any of his father's idiosyncrasies demanded. From the day that ceremonial cigars had been handed out with a bountiful flourish, Timothy had inspired his father to elaborate his happiness in formal terms. It was for his sake that Archibald lectured by the fireside for hours, that he gave voice to all his private moral constructions.

"Timothy, sit here on my lap. There's a good boy. I shall tell you about our Queen."

Lily listened too. His tone was calming, conversational and earnest. God's in his heaven. All's right with the world.

"The Queen is beautiful and good. Don't you think she looks beautiful in this picture, my boy? Her crown is gold, with many precious stones in it. That red one is a ruby.

"She is head of our Church, Timothy, the very top, just as the crown is at the very top of the Queen."

Timothy laughed, even though Archibald had not intended to amuse him. He patted his boy's head and went on. "It is called the Church of England, where we go to pray on Sunday. Good, Timothy! Yes, this is England, same as the Church. You are quite correct in noticing that. And we, Timothy, you and I, are Englishmen.

"Yes, my love, it is England everywhere we roam, in your room, in the fields, and yes," he smiled at Timothy's suggestion, "even on the treetop.

"What? Oh, yes, darling, you're quite right, we have not only Queens but Kings. Some day, we shall have one again. No, darling," said Archibald, laughing, "I am not going to be the King!" He drew his baby up into his arms and kissed his brow.

"Lily, would you like a sherry? Perhaps we'll all have a wee dram." Peter wandered in and out, ignoring his stepfather and giving Lily looks that said: what a royal arse.

"Well, now," continued Archibald, "Timothy seems to want a taste of sherry as well. All right, darling, you may have a sip of mine, a small bitty one, but then we must say our prayers, mustn't we, and go to bed."

Usually, Timothy coyly resisted bedtime. His wriggling and whine were always followed by a luxurious limpness when his father folded him tenderly in his arms and plodded up the stairs. If Archibald had been a touch less exact, their love would have lacked its ritual completeness. It was flawless, within and without, constant and unblushing. As for the offers of sherry, these were but the meekest emblem of Archibald's role. It was his way to unwrap towering canisters of Glenfiddich and be-ribboned boxes of Bombay Gin in the Christmas season, and make a nightly offering of either (just before Cook rang the bell for dinner). Lily learned that these treats, along with after-dinner mints, candied violets, and powdery Turkish Delight, were offered in the spirit of *noblesse oblige*. Being the head of a household had made Archibald noble. Holding out a tissued box of Belgian chocolates, the father's pride was that of the hunter with his catch: he had brought down a Christmas that stuck to the ribs. Timothy would never forget a Christmas spent under his Daddy's impenetrable roof.

And only a few years ago, this man was completely alone, thought Lily, discovering the wonderful liqueur secreted in her bon-bon.

10

THREE DAYS LATER, Julian arrived in Gloucestershire. He spotted Lily ambling alone in the countryside and watched her for a while. She seemed absorbed and happy. She was wonderful to look at.

He yelled out suddenly: "Startle easily?"

She jumped up in the air, and then she saw him.

He laughed aloud at the pretty confusion in her face.

She joined him, laughing.

"The famous Julian."

He nodded. She extended her hand in mock formality, as though wanting a handshake. He gripped it in his, then snaked his fingers through hers. Looking at his face, she tightened her own grip.

The wild horse she'd seen before was running in the distance; she grew conscious of the faint thundering of its hooves. It was running toward them, she thought.

She turned her head and saw it galloping. It was looking at them. She looked at Julian. He seemed perfectly calm. She looked back at the horse. It was galloping closer and closer.

"Aren't you scared?" she said. Julian felt her tense through the arm, and pulled her toward him, pressed her head down against his chest, and blinkered her eyes with his free hand.

"Mm hm," he answered.

She felt his heart pounding through his coat. He smelled wonderful, of the frost and the smoke and the bracken. Opening her eyes, she could see only the weave of his tweed and one leather button. His hand against her face smelled like soap, and the parted fingers made the world seem rose-orange. She didn't care what the horse did.

It had slowed to an amiable trot, and was circling around them. Innocently, as though to say: "Who, me? Scare you? Just playing!"

Julian stretched out a hand to the horse and patted its head. It wasn't a wild horse at all. It was docile and plain. Its head was long and mute. Lily suddenly found the beast very touching.

"Poor little horsey," said Julian, as he patiently stroked the enormous nose. "Lily was frightened of you. Can you imagine? She doesn't know what a lonely life you lead. Well, we're here now, Lily and I. Break open the bubbly!"

"And pass the sugar lumps," she added. But she wasn't really listening. Around them, she felt the countryside envelop her. She could feel the benign spreading forth of rolling meadows, of mist-heavy trees and puffy clouds. The vague lushness welcomed her. She looked at Julian. He was different than the last time.

He looked at her with the eyes of a forest creature, illumined by a shaft of light. Pupils dissolving into pinpoints as he turned and stared into her. Round black dots that fixed her neatly, and his hair around his face like an ink-cloud. He released the horse and it trotted away.

They sat down by a little stream.

"You look different," she said.

"I do? I feel happy today. I knew I'd see you. Peter told me. I was really excited."

"You were?"

"As soon as I got home, I looked for you. Peter told me you were out on a ramble. I flew out the door."

"I wonder what 'they' thought of that."

"'They' weren't the least bit surprised. But you can never tell, really."

"That's because they're spooky old turds," he allowed.

"Well, Peter's all right, don't you think?"

"I love my brother."

"But he is a jealous one," Lily continued. "I think he'll kill me over you assuming there is a you to get jealous about. He's kind of possessive of me. Says I'm his domestic-but-not-tame animal."

"Too bad for Peter. He can go rot. And by the way," said Julian, "*I'll* tame you."

"Oh, sure, go ahead and try."

"I mean it," said the Boy, deepening his timbre.

"O.K., I believe you," she answered, her voice lowered to meet his serious tones.

"I *want* you to love me," he insisted. "Only me and forever. No one ever has before. Do you know why?"

She shook her head.

"Because I wouldn't let them in. I want you to love me, because you have a power over me. You've infiltrated, somehow. Did you realize that?"

"No, I didn't," she said, struggling not to burst with happiness. She loved his exposition; she wanted it to go on, slowly, deliciously, forever.

"I don't believe you, Lily. I'll bet you know every little thing. You're doing it right now."

"Doing what?" She was smiling.

"Making me feel . . . mad, sort of. I don't know what I'll do about you."

"Oh, come on. Stop exaggerating."

"I'm not. I'm not. I'm being more honest than I like to be. I've been thinking about you ever since I saw you in the pub. This has never actually happened before. It feels uncomfortable. I don't know what it is. I can only describe how it feels: I feel a warm numbness, and a sense of infinity."

"Glib," she whispered, listening for more.

His flattery made her pious, drunken. Love could be their private religion, their pure, untouchable credo. Her cheeks blazed as he touched them, and then she admitted, "You have that power, too. Over me. I feel greedy and anxious, like I won't have my fill. I can't get there fast enough. And there you are, looking at me. I'm crazy, too, Julian. Can you help me?" Her voice was naive and seductive.

"Honestly?"

"Very honestly. Put your arm around me the way you did when the horse came charging at us."

"You look different, too, Lily," he said, holding her in both his arms. "Not as tense. You look so . . . amazing."

They ambled around and came to a large wood full of skeletal trees, both standing and fallen at their feet. They promptly lost their way amongst the cracked branches, wandering inward, deeper and deeper, circling toward the center of the wood.

They happened on an enormous stump. Lily stared at it for a minute, as though it were holy, a Stonehenge. Then she stretched herself out, bulky coat, boots and all. She raised her arms upward, as though inviting the embrace of some universal love. Julian entered this embrace, his weight, like a burden, releasing into hers, and into the stump.

His hair was cold and black, and it spilled downward. Her breath rose upwards, to the grey sky, soaring light and free. Floating.

Bright, bright white wisps that met the flowing clouds above them. Julian pinned her down; the clouds drifted lazily by. It felt wonderful, the contrast. She wriggled under his weight, then lay still, letting it pour into her.

"Look at me," he said, raising her face in his hands and focusing her eyes on his.

"What is your name?"

"Lily."

"Are you sure?"

"No . . . ."

"Who am I?"

A moment passed before she answered, eyes wet,

"You're mine."

They began kissing blindly.

11

HERE WAS SOMETHING GOING ON between them, Mrs. Kendall was certain. Lately their low voices disturbed her sleep at night; they seemed to throb through the ceiling of the sitting room, invading her bedroom above.

It was so peculiar, their murmuring. Surreal, almost. One voice carried over the other, like a chant. Mrs. Kendall knew a great deal about plainsong from listening to Archibald's explanation of it to Timothy. The sound was never abandoned to die. If a few monks should happen to grow short of breath (and with this she sympathized; Mrs. Kendall smoked cigarettes in endless chains), a few others lifted up their foundering note, and then they too were relieved, on and on, in alternation, forever. Endless. Endless!

Julian was developing large dark rings under his eyes. Did either of them ever sleep? Sometimes she peered, undetected, through the large glass sitting room doors. Her boy seemed so odd around Lily. He bit his nails to the quick; he flushed; he looked relieved and giggled; his eyes darted; he clasped his knees to his chin and wiggled an ankle. It was a wrenching sight for a mother to see. In the end, he was comfortless. The girl made him nervous. Once she saw him fall to his knees at Lily's feet and offer his beautiful head to the mercy of her hands. And he had been crying. But Julian never cried! The girl had slowly circled each eye with one slender finger.

Mrs. Kendall went into the kitchen, lit a cigarette and stirred her tea. She suffered from this awful insomnia, but couldn't the children get things done in daylight? It was as though the house had changed hands, with Lily its new mistress. *I'd* rather like to sit by the fire right now, she thought, staring at her dull grey tea under bulb light. Once she had come in to offer them some nice, dark fruitcake, but Lily had smilingly declined, and Julian had gazed at her like a mooncalf. Archibald could sleep through all of this, but she could not, she was afraid. His methodical snores nearly drowned out all that was happening below, but between the snores she could hear them so well that the fire nearly crackled in her hair.

Julian had always been the problem child. Peter was studious, even if he did need to get the better of everyone else and to have the last word. But Julian was the more sensitive. What didn't he see from the very moment he breathed life? (He wasn't a bit like Timothy, who took in just precisely what Archibald told him, and nothing more.) Julian had been a magical sort of child, like the creatures in fairy tales who sense the things that made you heart-weary. The magic horse with immortal head, and the magic Russian doll who spoke; oh, he and she had read them all together, hadn't they? But he was indecisive too, and sometimes lazy, so lazy that he had fits of it, kicking at the rug for his own inertia. Of course Peter was going to finish his puzzles if Julian gave up in the middle. Why did he always lose heart so easily?

He was always being swept along. His passivity made people persistent; he made them ravenous . . .. Scarcely twenty, he looked years older, with his long strong legs and back, and his hard chin cleft like the devil's foot. This had brought on the plague of girls and the flattery. He had broken some girl's heart already; there was a photograph of a skinny girl laying her head tentatively on his shoulder. That was the girl who had sent all the notes, probably, a full shoebox that, when removed for closet cleaning, had exhaled the scent of old violets. Julian had not seemed much altered by this affair. He was very given, though, to vanity, rearranging his father's old bow ties on his neck (these festoons filled a drawer), dangling a cigarette from his lips, fixing the mirror with that insolent grin.

And now Oxford had rejected him. It was hard, with one boy in, and the other left out in the cold. It was hard, hearing Julian's sour comments, comments that Peter himself might have made. "City of dreaming poofters." "Black gowns and underaged buggery." He couldn't stand not being wanted. How clever of this girl to want him utterly, to step in just now and exploit his torment.

Mrs. Kendall thought of Lily's finger, tracing the lines of her son's rending face. The girl was surely older than he. She'd studied. She'd traveled. Quite energetic, wasn't she? He was quite taken by it, in any case. Or being taken. Roughly opened. Trampled so the juices flowed. She certainly wasn't lazy. Said she had glandular fever, but it hadn't felled her. She slouched a bit and was often sighing, but that was the extent of its toll. Besides, Jews always sighed. Caught up in their greedy yearnings. A portable people, the Jews. Always coming from heaven knows where. Fragile as dandelions, as impossible to get rid of. Tough, too. Planted in your sitting room. This siren plainsong could go on forever, with or without support.

Helena Kendall stood by her thick glass doors. The fire had gutted; only a few embers glowed. In the arms of Julian lay Lily, curled up very small. He was stroking her hair, looking down into her eyes, and mumbling quietly. Lily made a little sound, and reached to be closer, like a newborn at the teat. Julian bent his head downward toward an engulfing, dark silence and remained. His mother, after a long instant, turned herself toward the stairway.

12

I N TRUTH, it was not just the sitting room that Lily had usurped. Mrs. Kendall's pantry teemed with the various jams she had captured in summer: gooseberry, strawberry, quince. These were perfect now, on hunks of her fresh-baked bread, at small hours, in the company of Julian. Lily had developed an enormous appetite in this house, and Julian's grew sympathetically. He had never gorged, had never had so much the sensation that he was feasting.

They never ate in haste. They did not, with greedy fists, fling great gobs into their mouths. There was, instead, an air of earnest play about these secret meals, an elfin atmosphere in which work and play, fantasy and engineering, were deftly confused. They sawed on their crusts, groaning with a humorous heaviness, as soft powder dusted them white. Massy stickiness was mortared on layer after layer, slice after slice. Thus they built something, together, at the large wooden table of the Kendall home. It was their altar.

Their meals were always taken in the quick of night, in silence. Different words might have been exchanged at different times, their feelings might have grown deeper with every night's passage, but the large wooden table was still and serene and constant. Winter was outside them, and a slumbering house around, but life was there, on the spot, with bread, and jam.

The table would be covered with a bright white glow, the moon peeping in through the darkness. Spot-lit hands fluttered toward mouths into darkness, then met, stroking slowly in the light. The world was safe, warm and glowing. Clocks could be heard ticking, a muffled, hibernatory sound. The house, in its dreaming, seemed close, a navy cape thrown over the two sleepwalkers it protected. Lily and Julian whispered when they spoke, but soon grasped that the night could insulate them completely. There was no need to modulate, no need to hide.

"Have you been wandering, too, Julian? I feel like a wandering Jew . . .." Her voice was uninflected by worry. She was spilling over, lolling in the soul.

"I'll wander with you," he answered, rocking her. They were adrift together on the rolling seas. He rocked her far more slowly than the quick tick-tock of clocks. Even the big wooden grandfather clock seemed hasty now; Julian's rhythm made time swell with a vast bounty.

I have all the time in the world, she thought, languidly. All the time in the whole, whole world. I can strain my gaze forever, until the figures on the pier are not just thumb-sized but invisible, all gone. And there's time in what's invisible, too. It rests there.

And still Julian rocked her, until he himself had disappeared to Lily, and all that remained was the rocking itself, and then sleep. The grandfather clock suddenly thought of something to say; it tolled: Bonnngggg . . .. Bonnngggg . . .. Bonnngggg . . ..

He scooped up the girl whose consciousness amazed him, and felt the sheer weight of her dead frame. Now she was unassuming. Her head fell back as he hoisted her aloft, fully exposing her white neck. It poured from the yoke of her dress like sand from an hourglass. Her bare feet tipped downward, her fingertips dangled, grazing, at his knees. He stood for a moment, absorbed by the shadow the moonlight cast on the wall.

The night began to lift. Julian raised Lily's head and watched her fluttering lids, pink under the rising sun. He sank his mouth upon hers, tasting hot berries. She bit him suddenly, knowingly, a small nip. Her legs kicked in tiny kicks in the air. She was half-heartedly searching for gravity. His arms felt strong.

He took her to the brightening window; they stared outwards together. The brilliant seal of the horizon stretched across their silent, awed faces.

13

APART FROM LILY, Julian had few loyalties. He did nothing with resistance. He was very fickle, although this trait often came across as adaptability. He took advice from everyone, found something to imitate in everyone. He had all the time in the world to hear the other point of view. The other point of view never annoyed him; he was spongy; he could take it in capaciously. Little phased him. Though a certain passion shone from his eyes, it was not a passion for depth but for breadth. Nor did he tend to look within himself; Julian beamed outward, attracting the excavators all around him.

He had been very happy to work with severely retarded adolescents. This era had been a peak in his short life. The project had been suggested by one of his public school tutors, who supposed it would teach him moral application. Julian was set to work among teenagers who, like all teenagers, wore T-shirts and sneakers and blue jeans, had young bodies and spotty faces. The girls, like all girls their age, had breasts and long, luxuriant hair. The paradox of nubility and malady might have unsettled some other novice, but not Julian. He had thrived.

Once, during an outing, Julian had photographed them all, one by one. There was something chilling in the care these photographs betrayed. They reflected a concentration that could never be reciprocated, a "love," perhaps, that could never be returned in kind, it was so abstract, so combinative a love. Did the girl with the curly red tendrils (her name was Betsy) know that the bluebell Julian had given her to hold had matched her eyes? Julian had caught her as the bluebell grazed her lid; she was smiling as though she sensed the visual pun. But in fact she did not even know the word for eyes.

There was also a photograph of Graham feeding the birds. A flock had descended, gathering around Graham like autograph seekers. Graham had time for every one of them, and the photograph showed this. It showed him on his hands and knees. There were birds on his head, birds on his ankle, and a huge bird-dropping on his shoulder. A beady-eyed bird on the outskirts who lacked several toes and appeared to have given up in the competition for crumbs. And Julian had caught this. Graham's face was not too visible in the photograph; Julian, standing, had captured the scene from above. When the film was developed, Graham, completely apathetic to the picture of himself (perhaps because he did not recognize the top-view of his own head) smiled at the one of Anna, and would not let go.

The photograph of Anna was an accident, really. Anna was the most "normal" looking of the group. Julian had daydreamed, often, of kissing her, sometimes of exploring her body with the most exquisite care. She would probably not have minded, either: she was sweet, playful and trusting. But on the day of the outing, Anna had been in a bad mood, perhaps because she had dripped chocolate ice cream on her new pink dress. One sign that Anna was more aware than many of the others was her sensitivity to dirt on her person. Her mother had successfully toilet-trained her. Anna could even apply the word "dirty" in a broad, metaphorical sense, as an insult or expletive. Now she was muttering "dirty . . . dirty . . . dirty . . ." sometimes at her dress, and sometimes angrily at Julian, who tried to cheer her up.

He had propped her against a tree, aimed his camera at her, and made her break into a smile by putting the camera down, running to her, and giving her a quick, tight hug. But when he returned to take the shot, her smile had faded; as he clicked the shutter he knew that it had faded. The photograph came out blurred: Anna was shown with her head moving downward toward her dress, still looking at the stain. Her arms remained outstretched from the hug that had filled them, and with her lowered head she looked a bit Christ-like, fragile, thin and wavering.

Even with Lily, Julian secretly relished a self-image as a wolf in sheep's clothing, a dream of villainous tyranny, even as he caressed the soft-bodied woman he kept in thrall. She trusts me, he would think, nerves prickling with desire, and I could tear her to pieces. He fed on her atavistic nightmares, her worried mouth, the eyes that would not settle. Julian was no longer the victim of circumstance; no, it would be she.

He sensed his own wild and delicate containment. Would he feast on her, his prey? In the midst of a deep embrace he would shove Lily's head back and then, having contemplated her fragile skull at arm's length, render the woman back, squeezing.

A King may look at a cat, he thought. And be very much fascinated. Pocket it in his purple robes, make it purr at the pulse-points. My Kingdom for a cat, dear Lily. Would you like to be the cat, hmmmm?

Lily often kissed Julian with a passion he did not yet completely feel, pulling his mouth apart with her jaw, prying his secretive face wide open so it looked wondering, and perhaps he did wonder.

Then, going suddenly soft, she would let him prod her drowsy lips, hanging her head as though drugged.

He felt himself become a man of meaning, a participant in an old rite. Lily made him quite mad. He would show her just how mad; he would cram her full of his madness. And then, the yielding of her cool skin would appease his spirit, domesticate the fierce young Briton. It was on old rite, with keen new communicants, and an unknown outcome.

14

Europe, 1944

A STORY Lily's mother had told her used to wander in and out of her mind. The story took place in Germany. Lily's mother had then been a young girl, a teenager of about sixteen. Her family was beginning to disappear because it was Jewish: mischievous Karl, who played in the streets despite every warning of traffic, and lately, of Nazis, and whose supper had remained on the table for days before anyone had had the heart to throw it into the trash; tired, old Papa, who always grumbled about his bad back, suddenly packed off to labor camp, somewhere; Grandmama, whom someone had pushed off the sidewalk, who now remained listless and still in her bed. It was an orchestrated time, as far as the Jews were concerned, although between the cry here, and the rumbling threat there, many hours remained to be spent in a sort of willful deafness.

The only picture which had survived that time and made it to the New World showed an elaborately crinolined infant (Lily's mother) sitting like a doll, as was then the fashion layer after layer of petticoat, jointless arms and legs flung out by the photographer, who must have said a merry thing as he tucked under his hood, and bald, except for a sepia tuft. So Lily had to imagine for herself the pale, serious gaze of the girl in the story, the glossy coronet of hair, the decent pinafore dress.

Lily's mother had eventually been transported to a labor camp that contained about a thousand women. Her own mother was taken that same day, and they never saw each other again, alive or dead. The young girl was ordered to go right. She noticed, looking backward, that her mother had been ordered to go left, and was walking toward a group of old women. Old women: it was hard to imagine what sort of work they were intended to do. It could not possibly be outdoor work, for it was winter. Much later, Lily would imagine the death of her grandmother as sanctuary from the bitter cold.

Lily's mother was one of the youngest in the camp. Children younger than she had been sent off elsewhere. She had cried like a child when all her auburn hair was cut off. She saw it floating down all around her, then briskly swept up and collected. She asked the perfunctory woman official where the enormous bags full of hair were taken. "They fill our mattresses and bedding," said the woman. "You see how nothing is wasted." Her voice was raised, declaiming to the antiseptic corners of the room.

The girl toiled outdoors. Like most of the women, she was assigned to dig ditches in the frozen ground. Her naked head felt cold, and her thin shift fluttered carelessly in the wind. Each day, in the snowy dawn, a thousand bald scarecrow shapes emerged. They looked like neither women nor men. With no mirror, it took the girl a long time to understand that she looked just like any one of those scarecrows about her. But some were dying; some withered more quickly in the frost than others. At the harsh morning "Appel:" UUUUPPPPP!!!! Lily's mother noticed the limp slugabeds that had struggled to their feet only the day before. If they were not yet dead, but only ill, these women were taken out and shot.

Each day, the roll call consumed more and more time, for the pauses between unclaimed names grew longer, and more names went unclaimed. The S.S. officers, livid, would swivel their eyes left and right as the unclaimed names echoed into silence in the air. Soon, too many names produced this mocking nothingness. A decision was made: the women would be given coats. The coats would be sewn from scraps of confiscated Jewish clothing. Sometimes, the girl imagined, a scrap may have come from a threadbare portion of a Nazi's uniform.

"You see, Lily? They slept cozy on my hair, but maybe I put their clothes on my back." Here, Gretta would smile a pearly smile. "We were very near to each other all the time, Lily."

Lily had often pondered this concept. "Yes," her mother persisted. "Close. We shared the same crazy world. We were their shadow, and they were ours. When we had winter, they had winter. Near us grew the *Tannenbaums* they chopped down for their Christmas. On the holiest night of their year I was crying: let them learn to be merciful to us, doesn't their Jesus tell them to be merciful? And even that night, as women were dying, they slept cozy on our hair. They were always so near, Lily. I could feel their warm breath. I could smell their hands on my clothing. Very, very near."

The first time Lily had heard this, it had given her a strange, almost erotic shock, as though a murderer, asleep at her side, had let a senseless hand drift familiarly to her throat and lie there, weighing softly down.

"We were not told about the coats beforehand. They were in a large shack and we stood outside, scared. No one could imagine that something good was waiting for us inside there. The doors had heavy padlocks that the Nazis freed up with great ceremony. Lily, when we saw what was there!

"Some women, I don't know how many, became a little crazy.

They began to throw themselves into the warm piles. Rolling in them. Some pulled at the coats, ripping the poorly sewn sleeves off. Buttons rolled on the floor. The fever spread until it seemed as though the women were dancing within a large bonfire: coats swirled like flames around their shoulders. It no longer mattered what a coat was for, what the practical use of such a garment was, that it was supposed to keep women like us alive to work a little longer in the cold. Time meant nothing anymore; it seemed like the last day in earth; nothing had a sensible purpose anymore. It was a crazy freedom.

"If anyone had started screaming, Lily . . . . If anyone had started screaming in such a bonfire, I believe to this day you would still hear that scream. You would not be able to get it out of your ears.

"Somehow, I felt very calm inside. I could see everything very clearly. I even noticed how some women stood apart from the mass, hesitating, wanting a coat, trying every now and then to get to the piles. But they couldn't. The swarming didn't stop. I began to faint. You know, you notice things out of all proportion when you lose consciousness. I saw a trail of grey flannel. I took notice and I thought: this coat is the one for me. After all the swirling and the grabbing stops, there will be a grey coat for Gretta.

"All of a sudden, a big hand slapped my face so violently that my nose sprayed with blood. I could not see the face behind the hand; the blood flew into my nose, my eyes, my mouth. I felt a tooth go down my throat and began to choke.

"Then I saw the Nazi's face. It remained right in front of mine, hovering as I tried to catch my breath. As though . . . unsure of something. He looked like a shy boy who wanted to ask me to dance. He seemed young—not five years older than I was. It was so peculiar, staring into his face as he stared into mine. I remember his sharp nose, and little dark whiskers. I remember thinking—he has black hair like a Jew.

"I felt him put his hand on my shoulder. The other hand he tightened into a fist, as though he would punch me. But I saw he kept it down, by his side. We were staring into each other's eyes, and he suddenly spoke:

"'But *why* did you grab?'

"His voice was angry, but confused, too, and his face was lost, uncomfortable. He seemed bewildered. Why did we grab? He didn't really know this kind of person who would act so passionately. Why didn't we behave like machines? Why didn't everything go as planned? Why did so many women die of cold, and now they had to give us coats? I thought of how we seemed to this junior Nazi with his simple orders. We must have been a horrifying surprise. Mere beatings could not fix all this disorder, these surprises, these grabbings.

"I looked at the boy. He was trembling with concentration. He stared at me so hard, as though to fix his lesson in my brain. But I hadn't grabbed. What should I have said? I was afraid the hand would hit me again if I opened my mouth. But I finally said, 'Please forgive me.' He acted as though he could not hear my voice. His stare did not alter. Then I saw him widen his eyes. He was looking at my naked head, staring as though he'd never seen a girl with her hair shaved off before.

"Lily, if you could only see how pretty I was before; well, I was young and vain. I felt as though I had been given the mirror I had been missing. I saw my ugliness in his eyes. It was more humiliating than any slap. Suddenly I raised up my voice. I was also crazy, like the others, I suppose, and said, 'You don't even see that I am not the right person. I grabbed nothing! You have bloodied my face for nothing! You have made a cruel mistake!'

"For this kind of outburst a Nazi would kill a Jew as though he were a fly.

"I could tell that he believed me. In relief, I began to sob, covering my face with my hands. But just as I did so, I felt him move one step away from me. I looked up and saw him raise his pistol. He had a terrifying expression on his face.

"You know, Lily, I suddenly stopped caring. I closed my eyes and thought, it's all the same to me, just as it is to you. I am one of the ones who grabbed. I am one of the others with the naked heads. I had hair and I haven't. I grabbed and I didn't. I'm alive and I'm dead. I'm young and I'm old. Yes and no and yes and no and yes and no and yes and no. I felt like laughing at him. Live or die? A silly riddle!

"I opened my eyes to look straight at him. He looked at me. Then he raised the gun to his own head, hesitated. I kept looking. But he didn't shoot himself. He began to cry, without a noise, like this."

Gretta opened her mouth wide, as though gasping for air. Her eyes went wild for a moment, trapped with the memory. Lily saw the Nazi in her eyes.

"I thought about grabbing the gun from him and killing him. It was just a thought, of course. He wasn't such a good murderer, and neither was I."

"And then?"

"What 'then'?" said her mother, returning to her awful calmness. "You think he proposed to me then? You think we fell in love and got married like a nice Romeo and Juliet?"

"No, but—"

"Did he raise the dead from the earth? The nightmare went on for many more years," said her mother. "The nightmare is going on still, in me. Do you think I don't feel it now, when I tell you? Only now, over there, a forest grows from the bloody ground, and from there they cut their Christmas trees for their martyred Lord. One more dead Jew, more, less . . . ."

"But don't you feel better knowing that a German cried over you?"

Gretta cut her: "Only a forest grows from the bloody ground," she repeated. "And he's alive to whistle in it. Unless some real Nazi eventually shot my junior soft-heart for his moment of weakness."

Lily had always hoped the poor man had survived somewhere. In her world, such incongruous people were precious and necessary, lovable and even holy.

15

Europe, 1976

THE VOLUPTUOUS SPLENDOR of the holiday season had nearly hypnotized Lily by the time Christmas day arrived. Christmas left her to her own imaginative resources; the family had it all "under their belt," and did not need to resort to conversation about meanings. Lily's thoughts bobbed freely, a dinghy on the seas. It was precisely when she tried to see things through their eyes that she went furthest abroad, and away from their actual notions.

For instance, she tried to see Jesus as she thought they must, as the martyred child of God. She tried to grasp the notion that death did not really conquer him (it helped her to think of the Jews; death never really conquered them, either). She thought of Mother Mary. She'd been summoned by God to a strange yet homely service: to augment the universal spirit with the warmth of her female body, to sacrifice her womb to the powers that must be. She had assented. Shy Miriam, Virgin of Israel, eyes bright with pure trust.

If Jesus had sacrificed himself for mankind, why, so had Mary. She had said: if that's what is needed to help my fellow wanderers on this painful earth, then here I am, Lord, open to your service. Mary, thought Lily, was like Queen Esther, the Jewish Queen of Persia. Esther had begun her life unassumingly, humbly. But then she had been called upon. In order to save the Jewish people from annihilation at the hands of King Ahasuerus (who had been evilly counseled by Haman), she went before the King himself, parading her loveliness, and found special favor in his eyes. He took her into his arms and married her; he was smitten. (Julian had fallen under the same auspicious spell, thought Lily.)

They took to their Jewesses, as God took to Mary, and a vast forgiveness became possible. After all, love allows the widest, most extravagant mercies. When King Ahasuerus was in Esther's thrall, and she in his embrace, she told him: the people you are being counseled to destroy are my people, my flesh and my blood. *Kill them and you will kill what you love. Be merciful and love will be infinite.* The King listened and understood. He spared the Jews, and killed his remorseless advisor.

So it was that one fragile Jewess had redeemed her kinsmen. So it had been with Mary-Miriam. Even God conceded that to make his own seductive son he would need a woman's soft womb. He would not go it alone this time, plucking a rib as an afterthought. No. Now he saw the power of the magic vessel, Woman; in her, he could forge his mortal interpleader. A stern King needs his tender maid. This was not chilly old Adam's time. Jesus was to begin life as a vibrant quickening egg, warmed to life by his mother's compassionate flesh.

Christmas was the day of Mary's labor, the labor of universal love. She had a son so delicious you could eat him, body and soul, and live on it forever. This was called Holy Communion. The family of man would spare each other, and feast instead, together, on the son of woman. *Ess, ess, mein kind.* The Jewish mother coaxes you to eat. Eat, eat, my child. Eat my child up! But do no more evil to each other. Mary smiles to see you belly-full of her love child, remembering the sweet months when she was full and ripe. *Ess mein kind*, mothers of all children. And spare them, King, Father, God, for all are your godchildren, soft as the belly into which you entered so weightily!

Actually, the Kendalls did not think much about religion. Neither the specific tale of the birthday at Bethlehem nor the symbolic one of mercy for all was recounted, much less stressed. This was natural: one was saved; why overburden a sure thing? Why be undignified? Why be heavy-handed? Archibald reached into the deep pockets of European civilization and pulled out old gold: English carols, German chorales, Latin chants. The record turntable spun round and round in eternal orbit, marking the centuries of our Lord. Mrs. Kendall had (ages and ages ago) put together a Christmas pudding, preserved with spirits and weighty with luscious, somber plums. A single penny had been planted within, a "lucky" coin which now re-emerged in Lily's mouth when the pudding (really a sodden cake) was divided and served. Everyone applauded, and Lily flushed. This was the only matter gambled with on Christmas Day. All else was peace, and received with dignity.

The Kendalls had faith that things were just as they should be. In church they recited their prayers without taxing the words with fear or doubt or hope. They just knew. They listened to the Queen reciting her Christmas message over the BBC. The voice of the Matriarch was thrilling: kind yet efficient, trusty. "Right," said Archibald when the speech ended, meaning not only "correct," but "right as rain." Peter yawned and said, "Christ! What a bore; what's next?" Next was real Brazilian coffee, and the best French Armagnac.

The only disturbing thing that had happened that day concerned the girl Lily herself. It was so unusual that Archibald and Helena had stopped in their tracks at church on the way up to the altar. They had been engaged in the process of receiving Communion. She had poked him smartly: "Just look!" Both Julian and the girl were getting into the Communion queue. (Peter was rebelliously staying put in his pew.) Husband and wife gaped at the girl. How dare she make a mockery of their service! How dare she embarrass them in church, before the vicar!

Julian, of course, had not asked Lily to take Communion. He didn't mind if she did or didn't. It was all her idea. He thought the whole thing a grand annual joke, and chatted about the "yummy bickies" and "sloshy wine." Lily, who in a different mood might have felt relieved at his lack of allegiances foreign to her, felt betrayed, now, by this irreverence. The Jew in her was porous, a sucker for the spirit of the time and place. To see Englishmen, of all people, on their knees, like baby birds accepting what was put into their open mouths: it touched her. She looked at the kneeling bodies and bowed heads; then she knelt amongst them, and bowed her head.

This was her vow: she promised to partake. Beyond England and its church, beyond this country, this family and even Julian, lay the endless realms of mortal effort and immortal rescue. Messiah . . . Is that not what we are here for? For a communion in trust? She ate bread and drank wine. With eyes closed, feeling the ground warm to her flesh from the warmth of the bodies of strangers, Lily felt herself redeemed from this time and place; it was now every-time, and here was every-place. For a moment, she felt like Esther, bowing to her Lord, raised in his arms to a savior-Queen. She felt like Mary, Miriam, surrendering to the universal spirit of loving reparation. The King's arms were not stone; they softened, and embraced her. They took her in. Like a mother looking into a cradle, Lily recognized without sadness the fragile innocence of flesh and blood. Light streamed through the thin vessels of her lids from the rays behind the stained glass windows.

· · ·

Julian was right beside her. He tried to think about Jesus Christ, the crucified, and of the agonies he had suffered. Crowns of thorns and stigmata. For a second he thought of being paddled and ridiculed in school, and of the athletic evil of boys. They were like pack animals. He was glad not to be going on to Oxford, he was. Sick of the pack, and sick of playing the game. Stupid, sodding rules. What help was Jesus, really, in this cruel world? He'd lost out. A weakling like me, thought Julian. Why do they bother asking him for anything? He's the bloody whipping boy! Why do they pretend he's not? Julian squeezed his closed eyes, repressing his bitterness, then looked up forlornly at the Reverend Stout.

16

THIS IS WHAT LILY SEES in Julian: a noble creature, young, staring onto his own eyes at the looking-glass. A slow smile spreads across his mouth; he knows that life is turning good, as in a magic metamorphosis. He knows that she is watching him discover this. He is shameless in her gaze.

She makes a million unanswerable demands. There is no end to her questioning. He thinks before he answers, and he answers. There is a modesty to his confusion. A happy naïveté. He does not mind abandoning his world for hers. He entrusts himself to her. As he answers her, she finds new questions . . . .

Nervous energy with no outlet. And when it finds an outlet, when she is the outlet, he is grateful, adoring. He sighs out with relief at the feel of full extension. A lost, errant boy; if set right, could conquer anything. If not, would fritter winningly. A rare, dangerous combination. She will save him. He will save her. When she talks about the Jews, he is her convert, her Paul into Saul. He furrows his brows in adopted pain, in concentration. They invigilate the night. Next time someone tries to bloody a Jewish face for a coat, he will stand up to them. She knows she has touched off a chivalrous fury in him: her status ennobles him. Next time, if there is a next time, he will be there.

He has no practical plans. Nor does she. This is the kind of love she has always sought. Loose. Like soldiers of fortune. Loose. Reckless.

17

A FTER CHURCH, not a word was spoken between husband and wife about Lily's having been "out of line," for each understood how the other felt, but Archibald did find the lesson in this for Timothy.

"Timothy," he said, "perhaps you are too young to understand what I shall tell you today, but I would like to tell it to you anyway. It is a sort of secret," said Archibald (this guaranteed the boy's attention), "so you must keep it in the family. All right?"

"Yes," said Timothy, climbing into his father's ample lap.

"Now, Timmy," said Archibald, settling the boy properly. "We are Christians. Do you remember my telling you about the Church of England?"

"Rock-a-bye-baby," sang Timothy, sucking his thumb.

"Listen, my boy," urged the father. "Listen. I will tell you everything, but you must listen very carefully, and behave sensibly."

The boy was still and motionless; Archibald proceeded. "We are Christians. Our church is the Church of England. That is, we: Mummy and Daddy and you—"

"You my Daddy!" pealed Timothy.

"Yes, my darling boy. We are part of that church. And so are you. And so are Peter and Julian."

"My brovers!" cried the child joyously.

"Say brothers, Timothy. Brothers. They are your half-brothers, my darling, for I am not their true daddy, only yours, my love, as you know," he flirted tenderly. "Now there is someone I have not yet mentioned. Who would that be?"

Timothy sucked his thumb and thought. "Whiskers, fiskers?"

"Stop it, now, Timothy! Not the silly cat. Now think sensibly," said the father, and his son grew sober in an instant. Archibald's voice modulated ominously between familiarity and a tutelary discipline.

"I am talking about that American girl, Lily. The girl that Peter brought to this house."

"Don't like her," said Timothy. "Make her go away!"

"Why, Timothy," Archibald smiled, "be kind. Of course you must 'like' her. That isn't my point. She seems a nice enough girl, I'm sure. But she is not a Christian, dear." Both were silent together for a moment. "And today at church she did something that was very naughty."

"What, Daddy?" Timothy's eyes were opened wide.

"She took some bread and wine from the church, our Church of England, of which she is not a true member and believer. Quite without a second thought, she stole it, gobbled it down just as surely as if she'd broken into the larder. Are you listening carefully, darling?" Timothy nodded his head sharply. "She was a greedy, greedy girl. She did not ask permission, for she surely knew she did not merit it. She simply went ahead and did just what she pleased. Now mind, my boy—"

"Will she get sick? Will she have to take nasty medicine?"

"No. She will stay just where she is, I am sure. The world is blind and dumb; things go by without comment. Or punishment,

I'm afraid. But Timothy, mind. The Lord himself was watching, and He knows what she did."

"Will he tell our Queen?" asked Timothy.

Archibald went on unheedingly, speaking to himself now: "Thought she was very clever, I'm sure, one of us, of course, the upstart! Easy as that! Just like that, how very simple!"

"Bad! Bad!" scowled Timothy, smacking a fat hand at the air. "Med-cine!!"

"But our Lord saw, Timothy."

"And Father Christmas, too?"

"Yes! And Daddy was watching. All the time, your Daddy was watching. And now," he dubbed his son's shoulders with a heavy hand, "*you* know."

"Now *I* know!" said Timothy, looking adoringly into his father's face.

"Right," said Archibald, smiling easily now. "You must take a little nap." The hand on the boy's shoulder grew light, and began stroking it reassuringly. "Shall I carry you up and read you a story?"

"No more scary," begged Timothy. "I scared now. No more scary."

"Don't talk like a baby, darling." He continued stroking. "What is scaring you?"

"Bad lady eat me."

"Don't worry, Timmy, now don't," he murmured. "We're in Daddy's house now, and I shall always look after you."

"Read me Peter Rabbit," ordered Timothy.

Up the stairs, to Timothy's room they went, an old, safe trail. The child was tucked snugly in. The father burbled to his adored flannel bundle, promising him the very world. Timothy's lids slackened under moist, lingering kisses. Then, deeply stirred, Archibald read his son the familiar story of the mischievous cottontail on Farmer McGregor's carrot patch. A peckish, poaching bunny. The mean farmer nearly made stew of him, but didn't. Peter got away. The story didn't scare Timothy one bit. He knew it by heart, almost, and fell asleep well before the safe, predestined outcome.

18

New York, 1960

LOWER EAST SIDE, NEW YORK. German-Jewish delis, people, food. What a combination! The Jews flung out but still craving that old country flavor. Deli. *Aufschnit*: the word for cold cuts. They were cut off cold, all right. But they always found a way to remember what they lost.

You could have a slice of salami with peas in it if you were a good girl. But if you had it, you could not eat anything with milk in it, not with it, and not right afterward. The Bible said, "Thou shalt not boil a kid in its mother's milk." Milk and meat go separate. Nursing mothers to the right. The little ones to the left. Meat is dead flesh (we lost so many, so many, so many), but milk is innocence and life (I fed you so you would live to remember what they tried to do to me). Beware! You who tug on ripped nipples, beware! There's the butcher outside, everywhere!!

The German deli-lady dangled the slice in her nice, clean *Aufschnit* shop. The green peas dangled against the rosy salami. Green as grass; grass-fed salami. Gentle, gentle eyes. Nice German lady. *Ess mein kind*, she'd say, just like mother. Was she Jewish? German and Jewish were too much alike. *Ess, mein shepsele.* Milk and meat should be separate.

Ice cream sang from the musical truck outside. If you had salami, you could not have ice cream for hours. Only *goyim* ate whatever and whenever they pleased. They smelled of beer and parts of animals, the types of animals that would make you really sick. Suckling pigs, crayfish. They had no stomach, just a big bag. That was why they could murder Jews and not feel sick afterwards.

Thou shall not boil a kid in its mother's milk.

Which kid? Me? Which mother? You, Mama?

19

Europe, 1976

I'M NOT GOING TO KEEP BLOODY QUIET about this, Julian, if that's what you're thinking." The two brothers lay on their narrow beds, at opposite ends of their large room. "It's really unfair. I mean, I invited her here, after all."

The light was on. Julian was reading.

"So?"

"Apologize. And stop it."

"Stop what?" Julian turned toward his brother slowly. "Why should I?"

He arched a brow. "You're not in love with her, are you?"

"I told you what I found objectionable. I invited her. It seemed the kind thing to do. She's my guest, not yours. She's mine. I discovered her. Don't you see how it how it mocks me to have the two of you bouncing about each night, doing heaven knows what?"

"Yeah, heaven knows. Heaven must have invented it." Julian leaned back luxuriously against his pillows. Mmmm . . ." he murmured. "Soft. Soft as a bosom."

Peter could see that sexy black hair of his, streaming across the starched white cotton. It really wasn't fair that one of them had all the charms.

"Mum's rather cross about this, too, I can tell you," he said. "She's heard you traipsing about. Thumping on the floorboards.

She's complained to Archibald. We all know. You're making fools of yourselves. Idiots."

"Are we? How embarrassing!"

"Yes. You are. Go ahead and laugh."

Julian got out of bed, walked over to Peter's, and sat down by his bony knees.

"Let me tell you something, darling."

"What?" said Peter coolly, though he felt slightly threatened by his brother's looming heft.

"I am besotted by this girl. I don't know why. And luckily, she seems to feel something too."

Peter's eyes turned very cold.

"You must teach me some of your Byronic techniques, brother," he said. "Wait until the heat dies down and she sees what a cretin you are."

Julian spat out, "You never want me to have anything, do you, Peter? Well here's something I have, and it's beyond all your clever words. Why don't you ask some Oxford chappies what's in here," he shouted, jabbing at his chest. "You'll never know it. Go choke on that!"

"Oh, no, Julian, I won't choke on that. You will!"

He leapt up and seized his brother's neck. Julian slapped away at his hand. He was larger; Julian, stronger, taller. He smacked Peter in the face, slowly and almost lazily. Peter loosened his grip to protect his sensitive nose. Then Peter grabbed a huge hunk of Julian's hair and gave it a violent wrench, screaming "SOD!!" Julian leapt at his brother in a mad fury; they fell, crashing, to the floor. The handsome boy scrambled over his brother, pinned him down, and straddled him firmly.

"Now, look," he said. "Stop squirming. You're truly so stupid."

"God, you've made me bleed!" screeched Peter. "Look at this! What is this? It's BLOOD!"

"It's just a little drip from your idiotic nostrils. Don't be such a baby. It's hardly bleeding at all. Does it hurt?"

"Of course it hurts, you prat! You berk! Stop tapping at my nose with your clumsy fingers!"

"I think you'll live."

"Well, I just wanted you to know that I'm very, very hurt by all this. I mean, I thought I'd have some time with you during the vac. I hardly ever see you. We're brothers, you know: brothers should band together. And instead I find you consumed by whatever it is and no time for me at all.

"Now get off my stomach. I must tend to my injuries."

Julian dismounted, then turned his head. Lily stood in the doorway, wearing a pale blue flannel nightgown. "It's funny," she said. "It's funny how Helena and Archibald don't get up to see what you two are shouting about. You two could wake the dead."

She looked very pretty and rosy.

"Well, perhaps dear Hell and Arch are making the beast with two backs. That's a scholarly allusion, Julian. Perhaps Lily will show you the reference some day."

"Oh, be quiet," Lily said.

Peter lay on the floor, inhaling and exhaling. He dabbed tentatively at his nose. A fight with one's brother was rather nice, in a way. Old times.

"Peter, what happened to your face?"

There was dried blood on his cheek and upper lip.

"I was fighting for your honor, you inhuman whore!!" said Peter. "Because I know what's going on under my . . . . "

"Your bleedin' nose?" said Julian.

"Right. Oh, you're so very witty!"

Lily felt mildly betrayed at being the center of this slapstick. Of course, Peter would eventually speak up about her and Julian. But she assumed he'd speak up to her. Now, she felt outnumbered by the brothers. Even though they'd fought. Perhaps because they'd fought. There was now a private sibling energy between them.

"I sort of wish you'd included me in this conversation," she said.

"It's an Aiken family matter," said Peter, primly. "This sort of thing has been going on for years. We have sorted things out. I've decided that he may have you, so long as you give me your first-born. Done?"

"Done," she laughed.

"I do so love a family matter." Peter had gotten off the floor and back into bed, drawing up the quilt so that only his head popped out. It looked like a twin- handled jug, with flax sticking out from the top.

"Can I give you a slap, too?" she said, wistfully. "I've always really wanted to."

Julian sat on Peter's bed again. He had taken hold of his brother's calf, through the spread, and was trying to take a bite out of it.

"OUCH! Stop it instantly!" shouted Peter.

"Lily," said Julian, after he'd tired of his game, "you don't know how much Peter deserves to be jealous of me and you. If you only knew the victories he's had! 'Peter's so responsible.' 'Peter's such a scholar.' 'Peter's sure to get a double-first.' 'Peter's sure to become a don.' He was head boy at Harrow as well. Head boy! At Harrow!

"By the way, Peter, do you know what Dad said when I saw him in Cannes?"

"Don't tease me. What?"

"I told him you were doing a bit of acting, and he was amazingly proud of you. I've never seen him so proud. Kept rattling on about his acting days, and OUDS, and how he'd done *The Canterbury Tales*, and *Volpone*, and Moliere's *Don Juan*, and Shakespeare under the stars in the Worcester College Gardens. Wanted me to tell him if you had talent."

"Really?" Peter's face glowed. "Gosh!"

"I told him you didn't, of course. Didn't seem to believe me. Kept grinning sort of stupidly, the way you are now. Said he might even pop over to Oxford and see you in a play sometime. If you can keep Mummy away long enough!"

"You're making the whole thing up! I can tell!"

"I'm not."

"Gosh!"

"Do you forgive me for being so much more lovable to *les demoiselles*?"

"I'll think about it," grumbled Peter.

Julian began tickling him; then he tickled Julian. They broke down into helpless wheezing brays.

"Say," said Lily, "D'you want to go downstairs and get something to eat? I'm ravenous."

They were hugging each other, shaking with laughter; "Haaaah!" "Haaaah!"

"Hey!" she said. "You guys, get a grip!"

They ignored her for a minute. She was relieved and very happy when their arms opened up to take her into their circle.

20

THE KENDALLS had been invited to a New Year's Eve Ball benefiting the parish. Plans had been fixed long ago, so now it was impossible to have Lily come along with the rest of the grown-ups. She would stay behind and watch Timothy. Lily said she didn't mind. There was no choice.

The family now readied itself. Archibald was rubbing a thin gel into his sparse grey hair to make it go flat above his ears. Then he combed it with a fine-toothed comb. Then he wiped the excess gel off the comb with a handkerchief, crumpled the handkerchief, and buried it in his baggy pocket. He wore a heavy black suit, a white shirt, and a frisky bowtie of Highland plaid. His shoes were spiffily buffed, and sported fresh laces.

Helena's stockings would not ride smoothly up her leg. Her nails had been freshly manicured and lacquered; she held her fingers stiffly so as not to ruin the polish, but could not thus manipulate the wrinkles from her nylon.

"Archibald, help me, dear."

He was slapping "Eau Sauvage" on his jowls, a present from her. "Smack, smack," went his face, like a naughty boy's bottom. He mischievously pretended not to hear her, so cheery and vain did he feel.

"Baldy!" she shouted, annoyed. (He hated any nickname, this one in particular.) "Now I've snagged it!"

Julian knocked on the door. "J-just a minute!" panted his mother, as she ran about searching for her dressing gown. A moment later, he stepped in, awash in Lily's rose essence. Archibald wrinkled his fleshy nose but said jovially: "Roses in winter, eh? Heh heh!"

"But why haven't you dressed yet?" said Helena anxiously, pulling her dressing gown closer together.

"Archibald, you wouldn't mind lending me a pair of cufflinks, would you?"

This request charmed the man. He looked at Julian and saw, perhaps for the first time, his own Timothy grown to be a man. Humble and strapping was Julian, sheepish and ripe. Archibald blushed with pleasure at the sight of this handsome stepson of his.

He pulled open a drawer with great ceremony and extracted a small velvet box. Inside the box were two identical pairs of golden cufflinks, each engraved with a Gothic "K."

"One pair is mine," said Archibald, his voice rich and portentous. "The other is to be Timothy's, when he's a man. You may wear it tonight, if you like."

Julian dropped his eyes and gazed into the soft dark box. Helena watched with pride.

"Which pair shall I take, then?" he quietly asked.

"Either one," said his stepfather. "They are as like as twins."

Julian plucked up one pair and closed his fingers around it. "Thank you," he said. "It's lovely. Peter will be green." This flattered Archibald.

"Well, hurry up," said Helena, as her son left the room. "Heavens, look at the time."

Helena's head got lost inside her billowing blue chiffon as she slipped it on. A clever quiver popped it out, and another slithered her slender arms through the long sleeves. The pale gown floated elegantly about her body now. She saw that she was still young; peering into the looking-glass, she was not disappointed. Helena sprayed herself thoughtfully with scent, stroking her earlobes, neck, her knees, and the valley between her breasts. Then she wiggled her hips at her husband, laughing at his surprise.

"Let me kiss you, Archie," she prettily said.

He lowered his cheek to her mouth genially; she planted a kiss on it, laughing.

"Oops, I've left a mark," she said happily.

It was a beautiful red bow on his clean-shaven jowl. Catching a glimpse of his reflection, he joined in her mirth, chuckling as he wiped his cheek with the heel of his hand.

"We're silly tonight, aren't we, dear?" he said.

"I so love a New Year," said Helena, looking up at his face, still a bit marked.

Later, as her feet obeyed the rhythm of her husband's in a dance, Helena thought worriedly of that girl, Lily, prowling around her home, her bedroom, opening her jars and vials, trying on her clothes, sniffing about where she had no right to be. She did not share these thoughts with Archibald. Apart from the fact that Julian (unencumbered at last by her company) seemed to be thriving on the village maidenhood, she bitterly regretted having left the audacious girl to her own devices. That one needs watching, she thought. That one needs minding. I'll bet she's twisting on my sheets this very moment, dreaming of my boy.

She watched Julian whirl across the dance floor, a garland of daisies (Nicola) in his arms. Nicola was throwing her head back, blond hair flying, face hectic with pleasure. Just dream, Lily, thought Helena, excitedly cruel. While here's the very flesh and blood you dream of, dancing away from you, at a party, under my watchful eyes.

21

TIMOTHY, in his yellow flannel pajamas, lounged in the sitting room by the fire, with Whisk plumply perched at his feet. Archibald had set the radio station to BBC3 before leaving; this was their favorite. Classic after graceful classic, punctuated by the basso profundo of the learned moderator. Timothy, lolling sensuously on his back and lost in melodies, waggled his toes. He pulled at his thumb with his lips and caressed it with his tongue; the music cascaded over him. His eyes were open but he did not look at the ceiling at which they were aimed. Nor did he seem to take notice of Lily's footsteps overhead.

Lily paced between her own room and the master bedroom. She was tired of brooding on her bed about the party at which she had not been welcome. The pillager's thrill that the house now provided diminished her sense of deprivation; now it was all hers. It took her a short while to work up the courage, but in the end, she lay on the Kendall bed, rollicking in the heady warmth of someone else's parents. She felt uncannily at home there, as though she had been conceived and born on that bed; the mattress sprang from time to time under her weight as though nudging her in friendly recognition.

She ran to Helena's armoire, buried her head in the diaphanous pastels that sighed out perfume, and prayed to be adopted by safe, lovely people. What a sensation a mother's touch was: the frocks felt like cool hands on her brow.

Helena had been a beauty, a heartbreaking beauty. Lily found a photograph of her in a drawer: long fair hair, blown by a breeze, a strand licking the shadowy space between her lips. The hem of her filmy dress seemed to be dancing in the wind. She was waving and smiling, wistfully hoping for joy. Her smile was the smile of the ocean-faring, posing shakily as engines rumble below. Helena was actually standing on grass, her slender feet encased in Grecian sandals. A handsome man with a black mustache held her fast around the waist, grinning rakishly at the camera. The waist tilted into the arm that grabbed it; there was a charge there. He bore a devilish resemblance to Julian; he had the same presumptuous expression, the same chin erotically cleft and hoist aloft, the same pale eyes. Behind them stood the boys, Peter and Julian, one a fair and gap-toothed little boy, the other a plump toddler of about Timothy's age. Julian leaned heavily on his father's muscular leg, his arm gripped about the shin. He was looking up at his father adoringly.

Timothy glared at her.

"Stop it," he said.

Lily turned. Timothy stood in the doorway, his face clouded, his blond hair glowing in the hallway light. Lily froze, hand on the picture frame.

"Why did you come upstairs?" she said, attempting to scold him.

He remained as omniscient and silent as ever. He would speak when he felt like speaking. His eyes did not seem to waver or even to blink. She had trouble meeting his glance.

"You eating and drinking too much! Greedy! Greedy! In our garden! Farmer McGregor come and eat you! Now you stealing Mummy's things!"

Timothy stared upward into Lily's nervous eyes. He pointed straight to the door. His mouth opened wide, the mouth of a dictator at an amphitheater.

"OUT!" he shouted.

From the sitting room rose strains of melody, infiltrating the void left by Timothy's silence. The music grew louder, clearer; she recognized it. *Ein' Feste Burg Ist Unser Gott.* A Mighty Fortress Is Our God. Ours, as opposed to yours.

"OUT!" he shouted again, his arm outstretched, pointing. The strong BBC chorale made Lily crazy. She felt dizzy.

"No. You get out! You get out!!" Her own voice, wild, screaming.

Timothy did not budge.

"I tell my Daddy," he said.

She was terrified. Tell him that she'd been snooping, or that she'd told his little boy to get out? His face told her that she was guilty of every crime, on the earth, and into eternity.

"Go ahead!"

She shoved him toward the door, not thinking, not looking at him, as though to look at him would spell her annihilation. His pajama-padded feet had no traction whatever on the floor and he skated madly. He fell at the doorway, unhurt.

"Oh my God, I'm sorry," said Lily, stepping over to pick Timmy up.

"No touch me," he said, standing up by himself. Then he pushed her back into his parent's bedroom. "Now stay there until my Daddy get home and he punish you."

"Hate you," he added, turning and going back down the staircase.

He took the stairs two feet at a time. Lily heard the final thump of his feet on the lower landing. She noticed the music downstairs again, an endless flotilla of waves and stops, of mouths and fingers. She stood in the bedroom, shaking with tears.

Within minutes, it seemed, Julian was grabbing her. She thought she was dreaming; he towered over her. He kissed her, laughing and kissing at the same time. It felt impossible.

"How did you get here—what are you doing here?" she finally managed to say.

His body was freezing. He told her he'd walked. The ball was half a mile away. He had ice in his hair. There he was—it seemed so suddenly—white shirt, burning face, tumbling black hair, drooping lashes. Drunk.

"I missed you so," he sobbed out. "Oh, Lily."

"Is the party already over?"

Then she looked at her watch. It was only about 10 o'clock.

"Obviously not . . . . Obviously, I love you."

A shade of pain emanated from his mouth; his lips turned down on the word "you," like a baby tasting something new, foreign. And a baby's surprise that the sweet world bore so pungent a core. His eyes peered openly at her, wonderingly. She felt an overwhelming tenderness for him. His ornate bow tie, stiff shirtfront, the sharp crease in his trousers: these dressed his abandoned self, his love-tossed image.

"Oh, Lily, Lily, if you should hurt me now, I'd die, you know."

They noticed their reflection in his mother's mirror. They stared at the reflection for a long time.

"You are so beautiful," he said, a trifle sadly.

They kissed again, and something passed between them, a painful intelligence each accepted of the other. Helena's armoire was still hanging open, and Lily went to close it. The fragrant pastel frocks swung like censers as she buried her face in them impulsively. She crushed them to her body, inhaling the sweet sweat.

Julian was just behind her, circling her waist. He pulled her away from the dresses; the armoire stayed agape.

"What do you want in there, Lily?" he asked softly. "What do you want that I can't give you?"

The tenderness in his voice amazed her. She looked at him. "What do you need, Lily?"

"Take me into your heart," she said. "Take me all the way in and let me stay there."

She let him take her over to the bed. The quilted satin coverlet was cold against her thighs. Julian's hands were up her skirt. He gripped her hips. Lily twisted luxuriously, finding each hard finger with her rolling flesh.

"Should I?" he said.

They hadn't yet; they hadn't dared to, in this house.

She opened her eyes. "But what if?"

"I don't care what they think anymore," he answered.

She felt him ease her skirt up, slide her legs open, and rest his heavy head between. His hair tickled the soft innermost parts of her thighs. She could feel his breath, acute, between. Close. He was staring into her blind center. Lily must have said something.

"Hmmm?" said Julian. His voice was thrilling.

She was thinking of Timothy coming in on this, seeing the two of them like this on his parent's bed.

"Timothy." said Lily, slowly.

"Timothy," said Julian, "is all right. I just saw him."

"What did he say?"

"He didn't see me. He was strutting about, down there, waving his fists madly, puffing his lips out, a regular dictator. He runs this house, you know. Got Archie wrapped around his finger."

Julian got up and tiptoed over to the doorway. He opened the door and leaned out, listening."

"Hear that?" he said. "Music. He's conducting his chorus. His troops."

Julian listened for another moment.

"No. Wait. Now he's talking to old Archibald. 'Daddy!' 'Daddy!'"

he imitated the boy's high voice. "Thinks he can call his Dad at any hour, day or not, and he'll come running."

"Won't he come upstairs?" said Lily. "He did before."

"He'll get sleepy soon. We'll find him on the couch when we're finished."

Julian was back, moving his hands and his mouth over her.

"He said he hated me, Julian," she said. Julian moved in a steady, domineering way that excited her.

"And *they* taught him to hate me." As she spoke her eyes filled with strange, unbidden tears. What she was feeling, in his touch, was as strong as hate. As great. An antidote. Hate was washing away, conquered.

"I'm going to show you what love is," he said.

"Can you?" she wondered.

"Oh, I will try."

His free hand wrestled with his spiffy black trousers. Lily realized that he wasn't "protected," told him so, and tried to stop him. She heard her mother's voice, chiding, "think with your head, Lily; think with your head." No mother, I can't. I won't. And he wouldn't let her, and she loved him for that.

"But what if?" was the last thing she said.

Julian echoed the sound of her words: "What if what if what if ...."

He struck up a rhythm with the words, swept her up in it. God weaves crazy plans in mortals. Spirits fantasize in women's wombs. Dreaming of what to be. What if a soul came to visit, made of their love. Souls come into our ignorance, having their say. Steadily. Traveling into the blind center. What if they never came home? At the time, it seemed anything but scary; it was home.

When at last her womb stirred, she pulled him inward, and he cried out.

An answering cry from downstairs: "Daddy!" Julian chuckled softly.

22

Europe, 1944

LILY'S FATHER had been married before. His first wife and his son were dead. A "righteous gentile" had hidden his family when the terror reached Poland. They had been given refuge beneath a barn. A storage area had been built there, and a few cracks in the wood floor were enlarged to provide them with air to breathe. Straw covered the hinged entry from view. Overhead were the sweet cows, whose mooing offered company, and whose brown bodies, precious heat.

Each night the old gentile, Pavel, brought food and water to the family and removed their waste. He never complained. These acts of mercy occurred in the silent darkness; only the moonlight on the straw illuminated Pavel's white head, hoary as that of a tired god, bowed to his huddled charges.

The cold was cruel to them. They could not get up and walk about to warm themselves. Their blood congealed in their veins. Only the infant boy could exercise his limbs in the narrow tomb; he stretched and twisted. The boy was a living hearth, warming them wherever he lay. He was a happy baby, ignorant of the world, for his mother's milk was magically right, and her arms protected him.

Then the mother became ill. She developed a high fever that shook her bones up, but for all the rattling she was never warm.

Even the baby boy draped on her body could not keep her warm. The fever persisted for a few days, and then lifted as suddenly as it had descended. The reprieve was short, however. With the next blizzard, the sickness returned. This time it overcame her, and her soul flew away.

When Pavel came that evening, he saw a strange sight, under the glow of the moon through the open barn door. A baby at a man's breast, tugging at the nipple and screaming with anger. The man's eyes were tightly shut, and he cradled the small bald head in one hand. He did not pull the child's mouth away from his breast. He let it make its demand. Pavel heard Josef speak:

"Try," said Josef, with a strange, sad smile. "Maybe milk will come."

Then Pavel saw that the Jewess had died. He pulled the dead woman out of the shelter and carried her outdoors. Josef could not follow. The last view of his wife: a pair of feet, silver in the moonlight. The mute soles of her feet. The dead mother of a screaming child.

Pavel cracked the earth outside the barn. He stood quietly, staring at her. She wore a thin shift, through which her breasts could easily be seen. She looked exceptionally young. Her breasts were still full, the nipples stiff. She smelled of milk, sweet and promising. He threw her into the ground, then threw the upchurned earth in after her, and crossed himself.

Pavel was frightened that someone would see him burying a woman. But what else could he have done? The body would soon have begun to stink in the hideaway. The cows would smell it after a short while, not to mention the two milkmaids who came each morning. Stupid they were, but God had given them each a nose.

The baby boy did not stop crying. Josef thought: now even an infant can know of horrors. Before, the world of men was crazy, but nature was not. My child had a mother. But now, nature has gone crazy too. A baby needs milk, and I am dry as dust. I am only a man: dust.

Pavel returned.

Josef said, "Is there any milk to give my son?"

But Pavel was an old man. His children were grown. Pavel thought, if I take the child to a wet nurse, there will be questions. Where did he come from, they will ask. The heavens above? And who is the father? Pavel, a limping old man? Who, then? God the Father himself? They will laugh. And why is this lad circumcised, they will ask. Is the little one perchance a Jew, a *Zhid*? That I could never admit, thought Pavel, never. They would kill us both, by the Holy Mother! He went into the house, and after a minute or so, returned.

"Here," he said to Josef, kindly. He flourished an earthenware bowl.

"This is cow's milk, but it is all I have. Take this cloth and dip it in, then put it in the boy's mouth, and he will suck."

Josef soaked the cloth in the milk and brought the tip of it to his son's mouth; the baby fed.

"Does it taste good, little baby?" Pavel coaxed, so caught up with the world under his ground that he might himself have crawled in to join the father and child. The baby sucked and sucked, and his father kept dipping the cloth into the cow's milk.

"These are good cows," said Pavel. "I raised them from when they were born, and sucked the milk of their mothers," he prattled encouragingly.

It would have been a wondrous sight to the soul of the mother, if souls look on: the kind old farmer, kneeling by the open trapdoor, murmuring to her husband and her boy, and the cows asleep beside them, and her own body, asleep outside, and the baby trying to live another day.

He failed. Did the mother see this, too? Did she hold out her arms and give him her breast to sleep upon again? Pavel opened the fresh grave and laid the baby down upon his mother. A tangle of bones.

Had Josef not been a learned man, he would not have been so furious with God. He remembered the story of Abraham and Isaac only too well; he had taken it too much to heart. God had told Abraham to take his son, his only son, his Isaac, and sacrifice him. And Abraham had been prepared to obey. But Isaac had been spared! God didn't need the sacrifice; God didn't want the sacrifice. He wanted only to know the extent of a man's devotion. Abraham offered and God refused. Isaac, his Isaac, had lived!

The story made sense to a man: God was only testing Abraham. So when the little boy had asked his father where the sacrificial lamb was, Abraham had said, "God will provide," and God made the words true. He had provided a real animal, and not a little boy, the light of his father's old eyes. But what was a man to believe when no ram was found? When the sacrifice was the precious son himself? What then?

"My only son!" roared Josef, shaking his head from side to side like a wounded animal.

After a while, when his anger had tired him (he was only human, and could not bear a grudge against God forever), he tried with all his might to remember his sin. He kept trying to remember what he had done. He kept failing.

23

Europe, 1976

T ABOUT 11:15, Julian got up slowly and began dressing.

"I'd better get back to the Ball before midnight."

They both thought this sounded like Cinderella's itinerary (jumbled) and laughed. Lily got up, too, straightened her clothes, and smoothed the bed. She felt its heat in her hand. She walked over to open the bedroom door, but before she could take a step, Julian had her back on the bed, and they rolled around, kissing and struggling.

"Your clothes!" she sputtered, half twisting away. "You'll ruin them!"

"Oh. Yeah," he said, acting very sober, and they both laughed at this.

He stood at the mirror, straightening his shirt, and reached for the elegant bowtie. He looked straight into his own blue eyes and said, "Lily, come look. I look different, don't I?"

"You do," she said.

Her face was as wild as his. They felt married.

"Do my tie for me."

As her hands rose up to his throat she couldn't resist: she wrapped the tie around his neck and pulled him down to her open mouth. She could have drunk those kisses from the old year and into the new.

The door groaned on its hinges. They parted, whipping their heads around, half-expecting to see Timothy wielding a birch rod.

"Oops!" said Julian, sniggering into his hand.

But no one was there. A chilly wind swept in. Faintly, the voice of the radio announcer: 11:30. Lily saw Whisk in the hallway, twitching his tail.

"Timothy?" Julian called out.

She looked at him.

"We probably should have put him to bed when you came home."

"He'll keep," said Julian. "He's been to bed late before." He looked just a tiny bit uneasy. "It's New Year's Eve, isn't it?"

"Let's go and see how he's doing."

Julian stood stock still for a moment. Then he descended the stairs.

"Timmy? Timmy?" Julian called out.

Lily stood at the top of the stairs for a moment, then flew down to join him.

Just beyond the sitting room where Timothy had sat, the door was swinging open, letting the world in. It was a lewd, uncanny sight. The wind blustered it to and fro; it moaned out protestingly on its hinges.

Lily took Julian's hand to encourage him; his stayed stiff and separate. He didn't seem to know that she was there.

"Oh, God, Oh, God," he wailed, "what's going on. Do you think he's been kidnapped?"

He ran outside, Lily following him.

There was hardly any light outside; only bluish patches of snow, and strips of ice flickering like lively water. A car passed on the dirt road, turning a corner. Julian ran out toward the headlights, but the car had passed. It was dark again. Lily wandered dully into the darkness, circling, not more than ten yards from the house. Her foot touched a warm clod. It was Timothy, face down to the ground. When she flipped him over, his eyes were closed, but he gave out a tiny groan.

"Julian!" she screamed. "I found him! Come!"

Julian ran over, and glanced downward at Timothy.

"He's breathing, but there's some blood, and he might be unconscious," said Lily, her voice coming out in pants.

"I'll go and get Mum and Archibald," said Julian. "You call for help."

She heard him run away, toward the New Year's Ball. The blood on Timothy's brow was thickening; his yellow hair was matted and stiff. She tried to lift him but fell on a big broken bough of a yew tree. He must have tripped right there, just on that very bough, running from her. Her feet slipped and slided in gullies of ice and snow. She sank down in the wet and pulled Timmy into her lap.

He was a heavy boy, and when she rose with him, they flopped down together. Finally, she made it into the house. She slammed the door against the cold. She heard her own voice saying, "Don't worry, don't worry."

Timothy lay on the sofa. There was an unflappable look on his face, a look of pure disdain.

Lily grabbed the telephone and dialed the operator. When he answered, she could not speak.

"Can't hear you, hello?"

"He fell!" she sobbed. "We fell in the snow!"

"What's that, Miss?"

"We fell in the snow!!" she screamed into the receiver, as loudly as she could.

Timothy opened his eyes, and Lily dropped the phone, meeting his stare head on. She could take it. His lips were pinkish blue, but his eyes burned into her. She leaned her head down towards his.

"I'm so sorry, baby," she said. She stroked his hair with her shaking hands; she cupped his cold cheeks.

"Can I hold you?"

He let her pick him up and put him to her chest. He leaned his head on her shoulder.

"Oh, my poor baby," she said, "I'm so sorry. Mummy and Daddy should be home, soon. Any minute. What happened?"

Timmy lifted his head and started to speak "I—I run—" and then, as though remembering, cried piteously and sank his head back down on Lily's shoulder.

Lily cried too. Together, they shook with sadness and relief, as though they were of one flesh and one blood.

24

J ULIAN DASHED INTO THE BALLROOM panting, wild-eyed. It was
nearly midnight; all the faces were silly and merry. He couldn't
find Archibald or his mother for a few agonizing minutes. Then
he spotted them. There they were. Dancing the tango, Archibald
seemed especially bouncy and free. His haunches jiggled as he led
his wife across the dance floor. Helena looked beautiful and young.
She held her head up high when she saw her son. She whispered
into Archibald's ear, and they danced toward Julian.

"Darling!" she sang out, waving her arm. "Where have you
been?" She threw her head back and put a long hand to her moist
throat. "Gosh, isn't it hot?"

Julian's mind played a trick on him just then. He thought not of
Timothy, but of Lily, beneath him, alive. He went hot and cold; he
went electric.

"Mother."

"Yes, dear?"

"Whatever is wrong with you?" said Archibald, beginning to
notice.

"Mother tonight I—Lily was—Timothy is—"

In a moment he would confess what he'd been doing on her bed.

"What is it? What are you saying? Speak up, lad!" said Archibald,
loudly.

"What is it, dear? What did you say about Timothy?"

"He's, he's . . . "

"Has something happened? Is Timothy all right?"

"No, Mother we've got to help him, we've got to leave!"

"But what in heaven's name has happened, dear? Where on earth have you been?"

Suddenly she saw it all.

"You've been home, have you?" Bitter eyes, bitter mouth.

It was an accident, thought Julian. The baby's escape and fall, the blood in the snow. The world was no greater than this: Lily, open and shuddering, soaked with his seed; Timothy, sinking into the cold silent earth. The tossing of bodies, this way and that. Accidents. A monumental groan escaped his lips.

"Let's go, immediately," said Archibald. He looked badly frightened.

"So you went home to see her," said Helena. "And now, see what's happened!"

She went to fetch Peter. He was chatting up a lovely brunette with porcelain skin and enormous round eyes. When his mother told him they had to leave, he looked terribly irritated. It was just before midnight.

Helena told him that Timothy had been hurt. The brunette's mouth opened wide with surprise.

The merrymakers looked up, puzzled, as the Kendalls fled from the Ball. But then midnight struck and they lost themselves in revelry. Cheering, hugging, hailing the new.

25

L ILY HEARD THE CAR pull into the driveway.
Archibald started shouting at her:
"Where's my SON?"

Then he saw.

"What the devil have you done?"

Lily was still holding Timothy. Now sleeping peacefully, he looked like an angel. The blood on his brow looked like sweet chocolate. Helena tried to grab him away, but Lily wouldn't let go. She slapped the girl's face hard, twice, but she would not give the baby up. Her grip tightened. Peter gave Lily a powerful shove and she fell off the sofa, tumbling to the floor with Timothy, who burst out in panicked shrieks.

"Damn her!" cried Peter. "God! Damn her! Mother, he's been hurt!"

"Oh, God," sobbed Helena.

They were all huddled over the baby, shaking him, coaxing him, begging him to stop crying. Their hysteria made him cry all the harder.

"CALL THE DOCTOR!" Archibald bellowed. "The boy is injured. Call him now!"

Lily went over to where Julian stood, alone in a corner.

"I did call the doctor," she told him softly.

"He looks better, Mum, he really does," Julian offered. "Much better than when I saw him last—"

"Saw him last? What does that mean? You were supposed to be at the ball, and she—"

"What do you mean he looks better? What happened?"

"He fell outside, Archibald. That's all—"

"Outside? On a winter's night? And what about this blood, then?"

"Did she strike him?"

"No, no," said Lily. "He fell over a stump. He might have passed out, but only for a second."

"Oh, God, I feel sick," said Julian. "I'm going to be sick in a moment."

He bent over his stomach, holding it with both hands.

Then Lily noticed an old grey man in the room, bending over Timothy. Beside him was a black bag. Doctor. He had just suddenly appeared. He hovered over the yellow flannel bundle like a vulture over a duckling. "Hit his head; heads bleed quite badly, but there's no need to panic," he said, swabbing at the blood with a quilted pad. "Here's another bruise, at the ankle," he continued thoughtfully.

"But his pajamas are soaked," sobbed Helena.

"He fell in the snow," said Lily. "He fell down and lay there."

"Good job he didn't freeze to death," snapped Peter.

He stared at Lily and Julian.

"Don't look at him," he said to Lily. "Look at me. You were the one in charge. You can't hide behind Julian now."

"I'm not trying to," she whispered.

"Speak up. Why weren't you minding him? You were here to mind the baby. What on earth is the matter with you?"

They all stared at her. Even the doctor.

Archibald suddenly began screaming: "But this is truly unthinkable!! Do you think there'll be any lasting damage?"

"Shouldn't think so," said the doctor. "Little boys are very sturdy, and they fall from trikes and trees. But they get up again, don't they? We'll keep an eye on him, of course."

"I suppose your type of people would be suing someone by now," muttered Helena.

"God, leave her people out of it," said Julian, nearly inaudible. Only Lily could hear him.

Timothy would survive; he would recover. Later, he remembered the incident as one in which he had behaved heroically, protecting the home from strangers at any cost.

26

"M Y ANGUISH was nothing to Archibald's."

Helena was talking to Julian. They stared at the fire in the sitting room. Lily and Peter had gone back to Oxford.

"He's still not the same man he was. He's always worried now. He won't let Timothy out of his sight. And he talks to himself, darling. You mustn't tell anyone. He talks to himself, half the time so softly that I can't make out what it is he's saying. The doctor told me not to worry. That he'll get over it in time. But it makes my skin crawl. I believe he's talking to the baby. Telling him to be careful, careful, careful!

"He stands outside Timmy's room at night, sometimes. Just watching him sleep. Staring at him. I know, Julian. I've followed him. I've waited for him to come back to bed.

"He hardly speaks to me lately. I don't get angry. I know he can't help it. If he'd lost Timmy it would have been the loss of his only son. I have three.

"And I can never give Archibald another. I'm too old. His whole life is that sweet little boy. There won't be another. Timmy's birth nearly killed me. I don't suppose you or Peter can remember how very ill I was. I'm not as young as I was when I married your father. Then I was as young and full of folly as you are now."

"I suppose you think I'm rambling," she suddenly broke off.

"No, mother. Don't say that. I'm listening."

"I feel you know me better than anyone, Julian. My own soul.

I used to talk to you for hours when you were just a baby. Because you have always understood. You know me better than anyone else in the world. I suppose you realize that. Did you know that your ancient, tiresome Mummy was mad about you?"

He nodded sadly.

"Don't you like a nice toasty fire, darling?"

"Yes."

"Darling?"

"Yes."

"Don't be angry—"

"Please don't, mother."

"I must ask you something."

"Please. I'd much rather you didn't."

"But Julian. It would be so much better if—I mean the way it is we're all confused about what happened, and if we could only . . . "

"All right," he said. "All right." His voice was cold.

" . . . unburden each other, darling."

"What exactly do you need to know, Mum?"

"That night. What—"

She stared down at her hands for a long time. Finally, a jagged sigh escaped her, and she covered her face.

"Please don't cry. I can't take it. Please."

"Oh, oh, oh," she sobbed.

Julian stared at her, his mother, breaking down. He felt a touch of disgust for her.

"What were you doing here, Julian? What were you doing while oh, oh . . ."

"While Timothy was alone downstairs," he offered quietly.

"What possessed you to come back here in the middle of the New Year's Ball?"

Now she was angry, dry. All of a sudden.

"What possessed you to leave the Ball and run, like a madman, in foul weather, to that girl?"

Her back had straightened; she glared.

He was silent. Thinking. He felt odd: he knew he would not speak until he knew. But he hadn't thought it out before. It had been vague before.

"I suppose I ran like a lover," he finally said.

"And are you still her 'lover'?"

"What do you want, mother?" Then, in a small voice, "she's gone, isn't she?"

"Thank God for that."

Secretly she thought: the girl is not gone. She'll never be gone. She is living in this world, and she'll be back. But Helena was thankful for the fact that Julian considered her "gone." He was not as tenacious as the girl; he had less imagination.

He did not hold on as well. Perhaps nothing could stop *her*. But he could easily be defeated. Thank God, she thought, for that.

They were silent. Julian thought of his own part in the accident.

He said, "Mother, I came home to see her. She was upstairs in her room. And we just, we just talked about things."

Mrs. Kendall knew he was lying. She saw what they'd done to her bed.

"Mum," he said, talking past her dubious expression, "did you know her own brother died in Poland when he was only a baby, and ... "

"And therefore you think she had the right to harm *our* baby?"

"Oh, Christ, just stop it!"

"Don't you ever, ever scream at me like that! I believe I've suffered enough from that girl not to be screamed at on her behalf by my own son!"

"I'm sorry. I'm just telling you things I know about her. Things she told me."

"Yes, of course. A long night of nothing but talk."

"Yes," he said, looking away. "We did talk. She told me that her father had studied to be a lawyer, but that when he came to America, he ended up repairing old books. Couldn't speak English, and . . . "

"I'm afraid I'm not finding this interesting, Julian."

"And her mother," he found himself rambling, "during the war, in the camps, you know, she, she worked in the kitchens, which was a rare privilege, under the circumstances."

Mrs. Helena Kendall was trained by Cordon Bleu, in Paris.

"Whatever is wrong with you, Julian? You're positively foaming at the mouth!"

He was overly impressionable.

He suddenly grew slack and exhausted. "I actually don't know what's wrong with me," he said, defeated.

"I do," said Helena. "You're infatuated. I know all about infatuation, although you probably don't think so. I've seen her kind. Seductive. Like your father. He was handsome, and dashing, and had been an actor and all the rest of it, and I was simply dizzy with infatuation. Do you know what infatuation is about? Lust. Blind, black lust. Not a very pretty word, is it? No.

"That's the sort of marriage we had. Attraction to something odd and strange and seemingly unattainable blinded me, got in the way of my good common sense. And what of your father? What of his great 'love'? I suffered horribly. Shame. Jealousy. Humiliation. I had enough, after a point. I sent him packing. And I'm not sorry. I am not sorry. I feel I've purged myself of a great and awful fever.

"Thank God Archibald came along to set me straight again. Your father, you see, stole my senses. Stole them clean away. That's what Lily's done to you. You must never put your faith in a love like that."

He saw how beautiful his mother really was. It was when she'd spoken about infatuation, about his father, about not regretting her loss, that he saw her as the beauty she tried to disown. She couldn't disown it.

Helena met her son's blue eyes. She saw what he was thinking. How like his father he was. No. No. Her eyes cleared and hardened. She gave a little busy shake of her head. If she'd had a purse she would have snapped it shut with a loud click.

She added, "Lily's older than you, you know. More mature. More worldly. It was easy for her to turn your head. Here you are, unable, I'm sorry to have to say, to get into Oxford, despite your very good brain, while she's there getting her second degree. She's been to University, in the United States. She's got a B.A. She has quite a cheek sailing across the merry seas just to put another feather in her cap. And grab herself a handsome Englishman like you, into the bargain.

"Archibald agrees with everything I'm saying, by the way. We'd spoken about Lily from the very beginning. He saw her looking at you, darling. He saw the sort of looks she gave you. Rapacious. Archibald's no fool. The fact that she's a little Jewess on top of everything else did not please him, I can assure you."

Helena stood up. "I'll say just one thing more. When you think of your lovely Lily, so brave, so pure, experimenting with her life— although I daresay it's ours she's played with—why don't you think of the life she's left behind in New York?

"Think of her parents. Those sorry, pathetic refugees. Those are her people, Julian. I don't happen to find it particularly picturesque. Do you? Try to be realistic. I have.

"The father: hair growing out of his nose, a greasy jacket. He repairs old books, you say? Well and good: think of the hands that repair those books. Calloused. Worn. Horny as a lizard's. His eyes, rheumy as an old Rabbi's. And the mother. How fierce she sounds. A clawed ancient. I can just hear her sniveling. Wailing. Can't you? An accuser, a Xanthippe, toiling over her boiling cauldrons. My God, Julian! The death camp cook! It would all be past hope.

"Why don't you look at me? Aren't you listening?"

"I am." He turned his head back to her, slowly.

She sat down beside him again. She put her arm around him, half-expecting him to resist. His shoulders were bowed.

"Darling?" she murmured. She reached up with her hand, twisting her son's luscious hair in her fingers.

"Oh, Mum," he broke down, with great, wracking sobs. A touch could break his heart; Lily's touch was so vividly remembered. Julian was vulnerable.

"There . . . there . . ." she said. He sank his face on her breast.

"Life is so ugly." He spoke it to her heart.

His mother didn't hear him. She kept twisting his locks in her hand, spilling his hair around and around her fingers. A miser in the counting house, grim with pride.

"I believe," she said, "that Lily seduced you up there. I believe that she seduced you on my very bed. But it doesn't matter now."

"Please. I can't listen anymore."

"Didn't she?"

"No. Can't you leave it? She didn't seduce me. No. No. No." He began wailing dismally.

"All right, darling. It's over. It doesn't matter now. She's there and you're here. It's done. It's all beyond our understanding, isn't it? Beyond our power to control." She leaned her head down upon his and let out a huge, tired, finalizing sigh.

"Y-yes." He felt the resting mass of his mother's skull as an awful imposition.

27

ILY CAME BACK to Oxford, and was surprised to see that all the rooms were occupied by strangers. The College had let them out to visiting physicists. She realized, with a growing sense of dread, that there was no place for her to stay. She dropped her bags at the porter's lodge and ran into Hall, hoping to find Mrs. Dancer there. When she saw her familiar face, she started to squall, as though she'd found her long-lost mother.

"Mrs. Dancer! Mrs. Dancer!" She was going into the kitchen, but Lily raced after her, scrambling past huge spluttering vats and urns and fryers.

"Hum?" She picked her head up high, listening. "Who is calling me?"

"It's me, Lily!" She touched the cuff of her starched white sleeves.

Mrs. Dancer looked at the girl kindly. "Leelah, dere is no College now. Why are you here now, Leelah?"

"Something happened, and now I don't know where I can go."

"You sit over dere now. I finish up."

Lily sat in the back of the gloomy, medieval Hall, at the end of a bench that must have been a mile long. It stretched right up to the High Table, where the dons sat at suppertime, decked out in their flowing black robes. Each chair at High Table was like a throne, with a high and elaborately carved back. "*Benedictus Benedicat,*" one of them would intone at the beginning of the meal. The voice would echo through the high, hollow vaultings. And the students would rumble: amen.

Mrs. Dancer came over and asked if she'd eaten.

Lily told her that she hadn't. Mrs. Dancer pointed to a place setting that hadn't been used, and told Lily to sit down there. She sat, among the physicists, and had tea and buttered toast. Then she went into the Common Room to look at the newspapers until Mrs. Dancer had time to speak to her. She had to clean up before she could get out of Hall. Then there'd be about half an hour before she had to start vacuuming and making the beds.

When Lily thought about Mrs. Dancer's work, she felt disgusting and evil and small. Here she was, traveling, studying. Wreaking disaster. Grab grab grab as though there were no one else in the world but herself and her little intensities. Mrs. Dancer's life was tedious and backbreaking. Day in, day out, no changes. It wasn't that she didn't complain. She did, bitterly, daily. But she had something real to rail against, freedom to look forward to. When she'd sit down on Lily's bed, stealing five minutes from a day of drudgery to chat (drinking coffee with three sugars), she'd glow with mischief and delight. Lily felt herself free-floating, spoiled. An agent of chaos. She made messes; Mrs. Dancer cleaned them. She filled the trashbin, all right; and Mrs. Dancer had to empty it. Here she was with an ugly tale to tell. Mrs. Dancer could only fit her in between breakfast and bed making. She had honest work to do.

When Mrs. Dancer came to her, Lily told her all about what had happened on New Year's Eve at the Kendall home. She told her all about Timothy, and how they'd quarreled, and how he'd fallen. Mrs. Dancer looked at her without surprise, but Lily noticed that she pressed her lips together.

"Are you angry at me?" she asked.

"No, Leelah. I was thinking about what you said. Maybe it's better that he get hurt, Leelah. Could be he had an evil yearnin' for your death. Could be he were your devil in a form."

"How would you know a thing like that?"

"I don't say I know, Leelah. Could be, that's all. You told me he put bad eyes on you all the time. It is a sign. Was always watchin' you, maybe even when you sleeping. And you tell me he talked with a cat."

"But a lot of people have cats!"

"A cat can be troublin'. Could be a sign. I add it into the measure." She paused. Lily began to believe what she was hearing. She would believe anything now.

Mrs. Dancer paused. "I sensed a danger, Leelah. It worried my mind. Now I see I quite correct."

"I can't stop thinking about it. It'll haunt me for the rest of my life!" Lily began to squall again.

"Of course, Leelah. Of course he haunt you. He be in your head, knockin' about, tryin' to steal your peace. I make you a mixture, Leelah."

She described a drink of berries and herbs.

"You drink it and you feel the peace in your mind again."

"Thank you."

"Now, Leelah, where are you going tonight?"

"Can I stay with you? I have nowhere to go."

College would be open in a few weeks.

"I live very plain, Leelah. I'm wonderin' if you will be happy dere. Still, you are quite welcome."

"Oh, no, you're wrong, Mrs. Dancer. I'd be happy anywhere you were. I don't need anything. I can sleep on the floor, even."

"I have a sofa in the sitting room for my daughter when she come. She's in London at the moment. You sleep dere."

"You have a daughter? How old is she?"

"Almost seventeen, gettin' to be a tall girl now. It's her daughter I be takin' care of meself, sweet Rebekah. Smart she is like a devil."

"Where's the father?"

"Oh, he run away, Leelah. He full of trouble. Drinkin' and fightin', and scarin' my poor girl."

She stared at Lily with fierce, burning eyes. In her determination to protect what she loved, Mrs. Dancer was wondrous and terrifying.

"Drinkin' and fightin', Leelah, like the rest. Just like my girl's Dad. I lookin' for a church brother now, to love me in my old age. Decent and fearin' God. Truth-tellin'. That's what I'm lookin' for, Leelah. Peace-lovin'. My devil-man, he burn my face with lye. But I throw de boilin' water over his head!!" She burst out laughing, throwing her head back. Lily noticed the pink-white skin which splattered across her neck.

"You did?"

"Mm hm!" She clapped her hands gaily and rocked forward and back. "I did scaaaaald him! Mm Hm!"

"Do you think I could come over to your house soon?" said Lily. "I think I feel a little shaky."

Mrs. Dancer handed her a key and directed her to the poorest section of Oxford, a section few students would ever know.

"Say hello to my sweet Rebekah," she said, her face soft. "She be sleepin' in her pram in de kitchen."

28

WHEN LILY GOT TO THE LITTLE HOUSE, she learned that Mrs. Dancer rented the downstairs flat from a Mrs. Jenkins, a blowsy, breathless, lavender-haired woman. When the baby cried, Mrs. Jenkins clambered into the kitchen to see about the commotion.

"Mrs. Dancer told me I could stay with her for a little while," Lily said. Rebekah stopped crying at the sound of her voice, looked at her intently, and began gurgling good-naturedly. Lily struck her finger out and the baby caught it up in her little brown fist.

"Why, you're American!" bellowed Mrs. Jenkins. She wore a tent-dress covered in mums. "I can't say I meet too many! Like the baby? A little bastard, she is! Sharp as a tack! Expect she'll be talking soon! Probably sound like her people! Don't hear many English voices lately. Hear everything but, it seems like sometimes. Indian, Pakistani, West Indian! Ah, well! I won't bore you!"

A minute later, she resumed:

"So! That's said! You've quite a large case there! In for a long stay, are you, dear?"

"Only about two weeks," said Lily. Then I go back to College. I've got a room there, but it's being used just now."

"Student, eh? Well, the world's open to you, then; you've got all

137

the opportunities, don't you? Have a seat, luv! Let me make you a cuppa tea! How d'you take it? Milk and sugar? I do!"

"Thanks."

She bustled over to the electric kettle, humming. Lily looked around. The truth was, she felt more comfortable here than she ever had with the Kendalls. The furniture was battered and sagged. The walls were papered with trellises of flowers: roses and daisies, particularly.

Everything was made to lift the spirit: the plastic flowers in the plastic vases, the wall-to-wall shag carpet, the electric hearth with its fake coals in their fake brazier. The chipped cup from which she drank her tea bore a portrait of King George VI. Frilly curtains billowed at the window. Nothing matched, nothing was in fashion, and all was neat as a pin. Something in all this naive effort took her back to her home, to the Lower East Side, where the fiats of design had been ignored, perhaps unnoticed, by her own parents.

Rebekah began crying again. Mrs. Jenkins snatched her up and plopped her into Lily's arms as she warmed up a bottle. The baby felt plump and sweet and strong.

"Nothing to them, babies! Had a few myself! Nice to be little, isn't it, have the world servin' you hand and foot! Ends soon enough, though, dunnit? How old are you?"

"Nearly twenty-two."

"A good age, I do say! A good age indeed! Youth is wasted on the young, I always say! You'd agree? Well, here's her milkies! Want to feed her?"

"Yes, please." Mrs. Jenkins handed Lily the bottle and Rebekah reached for it, waving her hands in the air. Lily looked into her acute little face. Cocoa brown, and fringed with a dark curly nimbus of hair. I could have baby like this, she thought. If the father is opposite to me, it does not matter; the baby is mine. Grows in me, takes my food and oxygen, linked to me by a cord of pulsing flesh. No matter who the father is, the baby is no stranger to its mother. Black or white, Christian or Jew: a baby, the link between strangers, between alien souls. A perfection of composition: halves. Half-man, half-woman: the birthright of the human race. Her secret dream was reconciliation, the dumb wisdom of married flesh. Seed-troth. Her own child could be half Jewish, and half not. All that spilled fratricidal blood, back in the veins of a living babe, coursing.

"What a miracle," said Lily, softly.

"Eh? What's that, dear? Oh, she eats like that all the time! No wonder to it at all! She's gained half a stone, I'll wager!"

Lily chuckled, then, without warning, began to shudder with tears. She felt astonished and ashamed, and tried to choke them back.

The last child she'd held had been Timothy Kendall.

Rebekah's brown twinkling eyes traveled wonderingly around Lily's contorted face, and her warm body began wriggling. Lily bent her head down toward her to hide from Mrs. Jenkins. She needn't have bothered: Mrs. J. was throwing pots around. By the time she looked at Lily again, she was fairly under control, and the baby was lying back in the pram.

"I think I'll make a nice hot stew for supper! Now, wouldn't that be tasty! Wouldn't it, now! Been crying, haven't you?"

"A- a little," she admitted.

"Well, then, blow your nose," she ordered, shoving a napkin at her. "You're all wet, you poor newt! How's the baby? Nice and full, I expect! She'll be wanting a burping, won't she?" She took Rebekah up in her arms. "Time for a lie-down, innit? Nothin' but sleep and eat, sleep and eat for that one, eh, luv? Shouldn't mind trading with her!"

"Would it be all right if I took a nap, too? Mrs. Dancer said I could just stretch out on the sofa."

"Right-O! Have a nice rest! It's a nice settee, don't you think? Always did like a nice pink! Have a rest! Pleasure meeting you! Fancy, all the way from America! Rebekah, say 'bye to your new friend!'"

"Goodnight." Lily went into the sitting room and lay down. In a minute she was fast asleep.

When she awoke, Mrs. Dancer was there, sitting in an armchair in the corner of the room, cuddling and singing to Rebekah. When she saw that Lily was awake, she said, "I make my mixture for you. I bring it now."

Mrs. Dancer stood up, shifting the baby to one hip, and smoothed the sweated hair away from Lily's face with a dry palm. Lily had developed a fever, it seemed, from the minute she'd closed her eyes. She spent the next two weeks in a not unpleasant haze.

29

THE FOLLOWING TERM at Oxford was a vacuum to Lily. She lay in bed, not reading, not writing essays, missing all her classes and tutorials. Her friends thought she'd had a relapse of glandular fever; perhaps they were right. She received worried, admonishing and threatening notes from her tutors, which she crumpled and tossed at the bin. The threats referred to the diminishing likelihood of her catching up with her course load to the extent that she'd pass finals.

Mrs. Dancer seemed not a bit surprised when Lily told her she thought she must be pregnant. She lauded Lily for having been in love with a man who had powerful "juices." Lily was amazed at herself and at Julian. They must have really let it go that night. For once she'd been totally open. She'd been stormed, endangered, and come out not only alive but life-giving. What do you know? she thought. The two of us added up to something, after all. Something bigger than either of us.

She thought that she'd better go home to have this baby. She would leave everything behind, she decided. Even Julian. It didn't matter if she needed him or not; he wasn't available. Had he ever called her, ever written? She realized that he had limitations; he was young, unformed, weak. Where had he been since that night? Safely at home, and not a word to her. He had gone, she decided, as far as he could go. Now there was the baby to think about. The baby was more precious than anything to her, more precious than Julian's attempts at loving her. It was the final and the only proof that they had once trusted each other.

Perhaps she was lying to herself. Perhaps she was furious to be alone and pregnant and exiled. Glad to have stolen a part of his self, a part of that family that they could not take away from her. Something she herself could take home to her own family. Away from Julian, and his doubts, and his fears. Away from the scene of her own greatest fears.

For Peter she felt something else, something very uncomplicated: she missed her friend. She did not like to think of leaving Oxford without seeing him again. There they were, in the same city, breathing the same air, practically, and they never saw each other.

She understood what he must be feeling. Apart from the horror of his little brother's accident, Peter must have suffered, at least in part, from guilt. He had, in her presence, made Timothy the butt of his good-natured wit: "Half-breed," he'd called him, "usurper," "fetus." The accident had made that harmless teasing, in retrospect, seem callous. And she'd witnessed it all.

She often thought of going to Christ Church and knocking on Peter's door, but she couldn't muster up the nerve. She wanted to be able to enjoy the sight of his funny, beaky face before he saw her own face and turned away in anger. The opportunity presented itself in a lucky way: a poster announced that Peter had won the starring role in Strindberg's *The Father*. Shelagh Eveline Fanning was directing. The run had started last week, and would continue through the next. She could sit in the audience, anonymous, preparing her nerve for a meeting. She cravenly waited until the last night of the run, when at last she bought a ticket.

As Lily sat down in the little theater, she wondered if Peter's father ever did make good his promise to catch his son's moment of glory. Nobody in the audience, at least on that night, looked as though they had fathered Peter and Julian. Nobody looked like the wandering satyr she'd never met but could vividly summon to mind, her baby's grandfather.

The feeling she carried around, that she was going to be a mother, did not really unsettle her. She didn't know why. She was animalistic, unintrospective. But this play, from the very first lines, attacked her nerves in a terrible way. All the squabbling, the desperate fighting for turf. She had read Keats only a few months ago. And he'd said that truth was beauty. But it wasn't so. Truth wasn't simply beautiful; the battle for truth was often ugly. She rubbed her stomach unconsciously, and listened.

LAURA: You don't know whether you are Bertha's father!

CAPTAIN: Don't I? [This was Peter!]

LAURA: How can you know when no one else knows?

CAPTAIN: Are you joking?

LAURA: No I am simply enjoying your teachings. Besides, how do you know that I have not been unfaithful to you?

CAPTAIN: I can believe many things of you but not that. And if you had been unfaithful, you would not be talking about it now!

LAURA: Suppose I was prepared to tolerate anything: to be an outcast, to be despised all for the sake of possessing and keeping my influence over my child and that I told the truth just now when I said: Bertha is my child, but not yours! Suppose—

CAPTAIN: That's enough!

LAURA: Just suppose! Then your power would be over!

All those angry words. Puzzles to her. Puzzles she had solved, or had forgotten to solve, or to which she'd forgotten the solution, or should one day solve. One day—though the knowledge itself could kill. Puzzles of history. Puzzles of legacy. Puzzles of trust.

The play ended at about ten o'clock. Afterwards, she wandered about town. She wandered up High Street and Broad Street, stopping in to have a drink at The Grapes. She tried to gather the courage to see Peter. She imagined him victorious, after his final performance. Blushing as he did when he felt delighted. Fanning would be crowing and glowing with the victory of her new protégé. Raising her arms outward and upward, beckoning him to enter, keeping a steady gaze. She'd grip him full around his thin body, hold him in her sturdy arms. Open her cape melodramatically to take him in. His head would be wedged between her breasts. She'd tremble and quiver; he would feel her heart. The light that entered Peter's eyes through that green cape would be forest light. He'd hear her chest rumble as she spoke, and hear the crowd's roar-laughter. Lost in the tropics, a star, amidst a chorus of chuckling creatures.

Lily finished her drink, and made her way slowly to Christ Church. All the way to Christ Church like a pilgrim, hearing the sound of her boot-heels clacking on the pavement. The moon glowed golden over the medieval town. The world smelled of ale and yellow stone-dust. It wasn't possible, it wasn't, that the centuries had died away. From far off, from time to time, she heard the "ring-ring!!" of a bicycle bell. She wanted to stay planted right there forever. To be entombed in the thick town walls where no one could ever find her or pry her out. Like the wishes people stuff into the Western Wall of the ruined temple.

30

WHEN SHE GOT TO THE COLLEGE, she looked up at Peter's window and saw a mass of exotics, celebrating. She plopped down on the bottom of his staircase and inhaled the warmth of the rotting wood. She saw the actors, one by one, make their exits from Peter's room. They had to step over her.

"'Scuse!"

"Pardon! (You bloody oaf!)"

"Passing through!"

"*A domani, Pietro; mio carissimo!*"

Finally, she mounted the stairs and knocked on his door. She waited a long time, then knocked again. She thought she could hear low laughter. Then a woman's voice: "No, don't, Peter!"

After a moment, the doorknob turned and the door swung open. A thick aroma of incense and cigarettes bathed her from within the room. Peter stared at her for a good minute, stony yet wavering, like a statue about to topple.

"Back . . . so soon?" he finally said. He tried to sound nasty, but there was a rusty note of hurt in his voice. He was mildly drunk, and looked very cool, wearing his sharply creased "Captain's" trousers and a fire-red T-shirt. He was sipping a Buck's Fizz. Lily looked up into his face and saw that she mattered to him.

"I've decided to leave Oxford."

He gestured to the bed. Lily thought he wanted her to sit there, but just as she was about to, she pulled herself up sharply. He had been pointing to Julian. Julian was sprawled on the bed, very drunk, an arm flung across his brow, to which moist tendrils adhered. For some reason, Lily could not avoid thinking of Steerforth, the fallen hero of David Copperfield.

Dead: she gazed at him as though he were a god.

"Julian?" she said quietly. "Is it you?"

His eyes were closed as though he were under a spell. On the edge of the bed sat Sabina.

"Drunk," said Peter. "Pissed out of his tiny brains. Seems he came up to Oxford to see my play, but he disappeared after Act I, as though he'd seen a ghost. We couldn't imagine where he'd gone, Sabina and I. That's Sabina." He pointed with a long forefinger. "She's my new Lady Jane."

"I've seen you, Sabina. I've seen you in The King's Arms. And then at the OUDS party."

"I've seen you," she replied, knowingly.

"And that's where we found him. In the bleeding King's Arms. We had the whole cast up here in my room, feeling each other's privates, and generally having a rather good time, when all of a sudden Sabina—did you know Julian shoved us together by way of recompense for stealing you—starts to worry. She gets quite nervous if she hasn't been soundly fucked for a few hours." He gave Sabina a kind look. "We shall remedy that very soon, dearest. So," he returned to Lily, "I sent her round to all the pubs, searching for the Princeling. And how did I know he'd be pubbing? You might well ask. I'm blessed and accursed with more than my fair share of brains. She saw you, by the way. Saw you guzzling in the Grapes.

"When I heard she'd seen you, I nearly became incontinent."

"Oh, I've really missed you!" blurted Lily.

"You're an imbecile. So where was I? Oh, yes, the Princeling. I'm sure you'll find that topic far more stimulating than the one about how you missed me."

"I did miss you, Peter."

"O.K., you souse. I believe you. Now let me finish my story. Finally, my darling located Julian in The King's Arms, and brought him tumbling home."

"Babbling and sobbing," laughed Sabina, her mouth wide open. Lily remembered those strong white horse-teeth of hers. If she'd ever had a crush on Julian, she'd gotten over it. She seemed on top of the world now. While Sabina filled the room with the sounds of hilarity, Lily caught a look at Peter's face. It was lonely and sad. He saw her looking, and quickly turned away. When he faced her again, he was cool again. Breezy.

"You were very good tonight, Peter. I saw your final performance."

So that was why Julian had run out, he thought.

"Oh, did you? How very Christian!" An old joke.

"It was great, Peter. You have a lot of talent. And you finally got a starring role! I couldn't believe it!"

"Finally. I suppose it's at least partly because I let Fanning stick a vibrating dildo up my arse. Eight feet long and ticking like a Geiger counter."

"No, really, Peter. You were wonderful. I had chills. Did your father ever show up?"

"Oh," he sighed, and turned it into a weak little laugh. "My father. Very preoccupied. Perhaps he doesn't fancy this particular little play. Reminds him of his long-forgotten paternity. Or perhaps he doesn't fancy this particular son of his. He's all gung ho to see

Julian in a play, isn't he, Sabina? Yes, he is. Real chip off the old sod's block, and recently discovered by the great Fanning as well. Apparently she thinks he has what Dad has: what they call 'shareees-mah.' Well, sod him and sod all the witches who fall for him.

"We all have our little idiosyncratic likes and dislikes, you see. I, for instance, don't like you very much. For example."

He had grown depressed and angry at the mention of his father. Lily understood. She knew Peter would always like her—here he was, sharing his insecurities. She looked over at Julian: was he listening to their conversation? He looked dead to the world, still.

"Peter," she said, "can I wake him?" Peter shrugged. She touched Julian's face and he grimaced, pushed her hand away, and loudly smacking his lips, turned over. His skin was very hot.

"Anyway, now we can be sure he'll be here for my next play. Dad, I mean. He's weak for Shakespeare. It's *Tempest*. Next term. Eighth week. I'm playing Prospero. Sabina's been cast as well. She'll be Miranda. It's sort of sweet having my nubile Nubian cast as the fruit of my loins. Such as they are. Shelagh thinks of every little twist!" After a moment he added, casually, "And Julian's got Caliban, the beast-man. It's a showy role of course, and amateurs fake it beautifully. And who do you think counseled him for his audition?"

"It's my favorite play, Peter. I practically know it by heart. I did Ariel once. In high school."

"Please," said Peter, pressing his forehead with the heels of both hands. "Please don't bore me."

He went over to his liquor collection and poured himself another drink.

"*She* nearly got Ariel," he said, gesturing at Sabina, "but someone said her teats were too pendulous for androgyny. Do you agree or disagree?"

"I totally agree." said Lily. Sabina looked her challengingly in the eye.

Lily took a good look at her. She wore a flamingo sarong and ankle-straps. Her thighs were strong and long; she had a lush, fat bottom. Her thick hair was made for tossing from side to side in ecstasy. Sexy as ever; sexy as hell. She gave limits to Peter's effeminate moue: he seemed to stop short and collect virile tension around her rolling flanks. Sabina sat on the edge of the bed upon which Julian lay. She looked like a lioness.

"Peter, I came to apologize to you. For everything I did. For upsetting you over Julian. For . . . "

"Yes, right. I understand. *Tout comprendre c'est tout pardonner.* And I do understand, I understand the meaning of it all, now that Sabina and I are connubial Olympians. I can only fault your taste, darling. Why do all you women surrender to such gaudy lures? Black hair and blue eyes. A broad back. Long torso. Strong thighs.

"Look at your lover now. Soused. Wept for a good incoherent hour, spoke gibberish about love, I think it was, then dropped like a shit-ball. I just pray he doesn't vomit on my shantung."

"Peter," she said. "I'm sorry about what happened that night. It was an awful, awful night. I'm sorry Timmy had to suffer because of my carelessness. If I could erase it all, I would. I wish it had been me that had fallen in the snow. I can't tell you how ashamed I feel when I think of how the baby suffered out there 'til we found him."

He turned away, pulled open a desk-drawer and fished out his cigarette case. He took out a cigarette; his hand shook as he lit it. "Well, look. Mum thinks you're a slag. Arch thinks you're the Antichrist. I don't think Timothy includes you in his little prayers at night. But I will always care for you. Strangely enough. Julian told me how it all happened. Look, it's all right."

She had suddenly started crying. He put his arms around her.

"Do you know what?" she said. "I haven't had a period in two months."

"You're pregnant?"

She nodded. Sabina gave a shriek that opened one of Julian's unconscious eyes for an instant, as though the eye itself had shrieked. Like a train whistle in the blind night. Peter did not immediately react.

"Are you sure?" he said lamely.

She nodded her head.

"I mean do you—are you actually going to have it?"

"Don't you think I ought to? I mean it's going to be some baby. Julian and I have pretty interesting sets of genes." She looked at Julian; so did Peter.

"Does *he* happen to know about your grand plans?"

"No, I'm not telling him until I'm ready."

"When . . .er . . . do you think that'll be, Lily?"

"After, after Passover. After Easter vac," she amended. "I'll see my parents, and think it over, and and maybe I'll write to him.

"I need to see them, you know," she persisted, though he didn't contradict her. "They love me more than he ever could, and only they can help me."

But even as she said these words she knew they couldn't help her out of this. They had risen to the Holocaust, but it had made them shy of hard, sudden twists of fortune. They would be stricken by the news; they would treat it like one more sighing burden. Mobilizing an old sadness, Josef would move tentatively; Gretta, warily. They would be her children as much as she their child. But there was the healthy, new life inside her to protect, too.

She nervously smoothed her round little stomach. It connected in her mind with the Passover feast, with the Matzoh-wafers. Every year, Josef explained that it was the poor bread that had sustained the Jews thousands of years ago, as they wandered through the wilderness. But one year, Gretta had said, "And the pious Germans wouldn't give a Jew a piece of Matzoh this big in the camps on Passover!" She had made a small tight circle in the air with angry fingers. Lily thought guiltily of the Communion wafer she had swallowed; that was the size of it. Small and round. But couldn't hope be small and round?

"Lily, what's wrong, you look dreadful."

Peter's voice was gentle as her father's now.

"Look here. You don't sound very sensible at all to me. Are you sure you've thought about this?"

"Oh, I've thought and thought," she said, vaguely trying to picture getting on the plane. She couldn't imagine flying with this awesome weight in her.

"Really," she said, "this is the very best thing. I feel too weak here, things don't go the way I plan, and . . ." Her voice broke off inconclusively.

"Peter, what choice do I have?"

"Look, Sabina," said Peter, "will you leave us alone for a minute? Take a walk in the quad or something. Thanks. There's a girl."

Sabina left slowly, and with a poor grace.

"Lily," he said, "I am very, very fond of you. You are the dearest thing, with your serious face and silly ideas. And Julian loves you."

He saw a tremor in her face.

"You take my word for it. My word of honor. He loves you. Even when he doesn't seem to.

"But we've all been shaken, and miserable, and things have gone a bit funny between us. I don't even know what's caused it. I know I shouted some very cruel things at you that night. I was a bit over the top, as Miss Fanning likes to say. I was a bit hysterical about Timmy. It's funny, maybe I love the little half-breed after all.

"It must be blood, Lily. His mother is my mother, and Julian's mother. Our mother's son. I couldn't stand to see him lying there like that. As though he were dead. I thought he was. It honestly frightened me. We're all brothers, and I felt it that night very strongly. But Lily, I don't blame you any more than I blame Julian. It was an accident. And if it was more—if it was a crime of passion—then I actually envy you for that passion. It's a rare thing. I've never felt it.

"Do you understand, though, why we've been so standoffish? It's a matter of blood. A silly concept, I know. But it's passed. Timothy's all right. It's passed."

She said nothing. She was thinking: no, it hasn't passed. The baby we're talking about, I'm carrying him. Your blood and mine are mingled; I walk around with it, and it grows strong. He's mine. And Julian's. And Timothy's. And your mother's. And still mine. And this life will be a Jewish life, because this time, I'm behind the "silly concept." I'm the one who's closing ranks.

Once, staring at the lamb-shank on the Passover plate, she'd asked: "Why do they call Christ the Paschal lamb?"

"Well, Lily," her father had answered, "You know that Jesus was Jewish. Fine. He had a Passover Seder, in Israel, where we come from. This was just before he died. So there was before him Matzoh, and bitter herbs, and also the Paschal lamb. Now why they call him a lamb is another story. Because to them his death created another Torah, you know, Lily. The New Testament.

"So they took the 'Old' Testament, our Torah that was handed down to Moses at Mount Sinai, and they decided that it was useless, like an old father you don't need anymore. And they stuck it in the corner, disgraced and forgotten. But Lily, the old person was not dead. The old person was endowed with eternal life. Because the Jews did not forget him."

"For our loyalty we have been tortured for thousands of years," Gretta had said. "In the name of that gentle lamb."

Looking now at Peter's lashless, puzzled eyes, Lily felt murderous. She was glad that Julian couldn't hear them talking about "Us" and "Them." She hated that xenophobic, bloody-minded feeling; she hated herself for sharing it. Personal love can be broken on such inquisitions. And broken, disgraced, like the "old person" her father had spoken of, how could it be remembered forever?

But then she looked over at the beautiful Julian. She had never seen a more miraculous creature of nature. He had thought her lovable. He had loved her in the best way that he knew, to the limit that he could. His body, too, had fit hers perfectly. They had made real love, in wild belief. His seed had taken on life inside her. She had made a home for him there. Why didn't this change anything?

A lovely, dreaming boy she had to leave. For good. She bent over and imprinted a kiss on his brow.

Peter came over to her. He held her quaking body in his arms. She steadied herself.

"Good-bye, Lily."

He waved at the door. She heard him shut it behind her. Then there was silence, and a hollowness, and a burning as she quickly walked the stairs.

31

Europe, 1977 / Europe, 1944

WALKING BACK TO HER ROOM on the cobblestoned path, in the dark of the night, the young girl called up Peter's voice in her head: Goodbye, Lily. Goodbye, Lily. Goodbye, Goodbye.

Her own name lilted strangely in her ears that night, as she walked through the winding streets.

Lilililililily.

A funny name. Tonight she hardly knew it. Perhaps it had never, really, been hers. Like many other Jewish children, Lily Taub had been named after a dead person, and not only a dead person, but a martyr.

Was it some dead soul, replacing Peter's voice in Lily's ear?

Lily's mother had been lucky in concentration camp. An opening (death) had occurred among the kitchen workers and she had been selected to fill it. What a sign from above! This meant that she would no longer be exposed to the cold, that the work itself would be far less exhausting, and that most of all she would be sure of having enough to eat! As soon as the news got around that Gretta was going to work with food, people treated her with special respect. She was now powerful.

The soup they gave her to ladle out was thin. At the bottom of the bucket, though, were solid bits. A piece of potato could save a life; so could a couple of beans. The question was (the question was visible on the starving faces): would she ladle from the thick bottom or from the watery top? How could she stand to look at those faces behind their trembling, upraised bowls? Almost expiring, but for the quickening desperation when her ladle began to dip. How they glittered, those eyes; how they flattered and cursed her, those mouths.

Eventually, Gretta ladled mechanically, feeling only a growing fatigue in her arm as, cooperatively, the bucket began to empty. She poured and poured as supplicants passed, a weary priest among whispers and wails.

Gretta's closest friend at the camp was called Lili. She had been a startling beauty when she first arrived, with a thick mane of hair and dazzling eyes. She stood, hands on hips, and stared at the Nazis very calmly. Her gaze remained calm as her hair was shaved away, exposing a great naked head. She held it aloft, as though it were an Egyptian bronze.

Lili was assigned to the bunk below Gretta's. During the first night, she had spread her lips wide and sung full-throatedly in the dark barracks. Her voice was low and it was strong, too; the wooden bunks vibrated mesmerically. Those who slept through Lili's songs were deep sleepers; perhaps something in the notes made them sleep the more deeply. The song was not familiar to Gretta, but she found it easy to understand, the way one understands a formless cloud, or the moon that does not always look, or have to look, like a smiling face. It was like birdsong; it advanced to no climax, and did not therefore fall away.

Not long after Lili was brought to the camp, she found favor in the eyes of a Nazi. In the daytime, she had dug trenches, her large legs planted apart like a trestle, flinging dirt over her shoulder so cockily that all the Nazis had taken notice of her. All the Nazi-men: they gawked at Lili, at her magnificent hips, working for them, at her beautiful head, ripe as a gourd, at her parted mouth, streaming with notes. She grinned insolently at them, never breaking rhythm with the hard dirt at her feet. One Nazi, among all, had returned a grin. Lili did not especially notice him; she did not focus. But eventually he made her focus.

Eventually, she lay on her back beneath him, silently. Still later, because he became a human being to her, and she, perhaps, to him, she found herself singing in his ear as her arms and legs danced upwards in the air above his head. Her hair grew back quickly, becoming downy to his soft caressing strokes. Her muscles softened; she never put a thread on them; she was ever on the bed, his ready infant. The man used to suck at her nipples, as though he had forgotten who was weak and who strong, who the parent and who the child.

She sang him to sleep, rocking her wide hips below. In time he threw Lili out. But not before every Nazi who cared to had degraded her as the stinking Jew-whore she was. Her man was in the next room, listening to the sounds of his fellows laughing in her face and raping her. He felt murderous; he had had enough of her; she was beginning to make a fool of him. Those Jew-witches get into your heart, he thought. He was getting soft as a woman; she'd bedeviled him.

Let her try her tricks on them, he thought, and let her wiggle those hips in the gas chamber. Choking Jews dance wild in there. Her songs and her smirks and her crocodile tears. I don't care, I don't care, I don't care, he thought, pacing the floor, listening to her cries.

A gang of men in uniform approached Lili to do the quick business. They stood on the edge of the rumpled bed and lugged her roughly to them, one by one, by her ankles. Few undressed. They unzipped, retaining their status, then zipped again, restored.

All of them having had her, one or two invented a new amusement. They decided to crush her face. One smashed her nose, the other sent her teeth flying. Her mouth collapsed. Her blood soaked the floor.

"Call in another whore to mop up here!" yelled one chunky Nazi, gaily hoisting his trousers (this one had stripped to avoid staining the fresh uniform). The bed itself was drenched.

Lili did not die just then. She returned to work. This was about the time that Gretta began working in the kitchen. Lili was unrecognizable, and could not chew the extra scraps that Gretta managed to sneak to her. She listlessly pushed peelings back to her molars, and then would forget to chew. Gretta learned to treat her like a baby: she chewed the food herself, then placed it into Lili's mouth, coaxing her with a soft voice, "Try, Lili, please." One of Lili's eyes could not open anymore, and the other oozed involuntary tears, and looked out with a horrifying docility.

"Lili! Please, for me!" begged Gretta. Where Lili had once stood planted by day, she now trembled pathetically in the wind, confused, looking down with wonder into the deep hole the others were busily digging. It was a mass grave.

Goodbye, Lili, goodbye. Goodbye, goodbye.

Lily was named after this woman, and not, as was the convention, after her grandparents, who also toppled somewhere in Europe, into anonymous earth. It was not that Gretta had forgotten her own mother and father. But when she first heard her daughter's strong, stubborn cries, she thought of the singing voice of Lili in the dark barracks.

Lily, winding home, sang out again:

Lililililililily.

She did not summon up martyrdom to Holy Wars, or martyrdom to love. She heard the sound, pure: a magical, lilting, umbilical
tune, anchored securely inside her.

It sang her homeward.

32

IN THE MIDDLE OF HER JOURNEY, Lily stopped with a jolt: a sudden instinct warned her away from danger. She knew, all at once, what her parents would tell her to do: abort.

The Lili after whom she was named had once been pregnant, too. That was a secret she had learned not from her mother, but from another survivor, Eva. Eva had winked and said, "Why do you think the Nazi threw her out? It was because she was carrying a child from him. Imagine: half Jew and half Nazi. Imagine. On the night he threw her to the dogs, she must have lost it. Or if not then, then later, when they put her to work, broken, in the fields again. No one wants a baby like that on this earth. Not Jew, not Christian." When Lily had told her parents what she knew about her namesake, her mother had responded: "It was not God's will to bind two enemies." Even her gentle father had added, "You see, Lily, such a baby goes against nature."

With all her heart, she longed to be back with Mrs. Dancer and little Rebekah. Mrs. Dancer would protect her from danger, surely. But Lily could not stay longer with the poor woman; the house was tiny, and crowded. Mrs. Dancer had her own daughter, who by now would be back from London.

There was no place for Lily to go.

33

J ULIAN SAT UP IN BED, sad and tense. The bedding was twisted
around his body like a chrysalis.

"She was here? In this room? Last night? Why on earth
didn't you tell me, Peter?"

Peter knelt over the electric kettle, and Julian couldn't see his
face. He was making coffee.

When he had finished stirring in the cream and sugar, he rose,
strode over to Julian, and handed him a steaming mug.

Then he said: "Because you were a ruddy, two-ton, drool-
ing cadaver last night, that's why. How much did you pour
down?"

"No, Peter. Why?"

Julian had no one else to plead to. There was no Lily in the
room. The fact that he'd missed her by inches and hours filled him
with an ungovernable sadness.

"Look, Julian, it isn't all up to me, is it? It's really your doing.
You were at the theatre last night. You saw her. You ran out. And
you got dead drunk. You."

"Well, you're right about that," said Julian.

He gave a little wincing toss of the head.

"Well, then. Whose fault is it? Lily's? Mine? And you ran out
before my best scene. You missed my best scene. It amazes me that

163

my own brother could walk out on the last performance of my first big part. My best scene. Ask anyone. I turned puce in that scene last night; I was brilliant! You disloyal pig." He was only half-teasing.

"And now it's all over, Julian. My play. You will never see it again. So don't you yell at me for not doing something for you."

He sighed out lengthily.

"All right. All right. You look shattered. You smell awful. You must feel awful. You're not even drinking your coffee, and here I've used fresh cream and demerara sugar."

"Peter, don't, please. Don't be funny now."

Julian rolled over on his stomach and dug his face into the pillow.

"Lily was here last night," he said, "and I slept right through it."

"I suppose, then, that you don't recall Lily's kissing you?"

"Just stop, Peter! Won't you?"

"I'm not being funny. It's true, little brother."

"Kissed me? What do you mean?" He turned around slowly.

"On your forehead. And you slept right through. Were you pretending?"

"No!"

"Frankly, she seemed to think so. I could tell. I pick these things up. I'm an experienced actor sensitive to the nuances, you know. She seemed a bit surprised that you didn't open your eyes. Hurt, I'd say. But she covered it up. She was very coy. As though she'd be perfectly happy never to see you again. But we know Lily better than she thinks we do, don't we?"

"I hope so."

"So. If a kiss couldn't wake you, or the manufactured shrug of your darling's coy shoulders, what could I have hoped to do? Turned you upside-down and let the drink slide out?"

Lily had kissed him. Julian wondered what she'd been thinking. Kisses could be dismissive, loving, condescending, sad. He wondered what she was thinking now, as he thought of her. He had lost the instinct of who she was, and of who she thought he was. The accident had done this to them. That was the embarrassment. Not to have spoken since she'd left his home in a disgraced panic: how had he let this come about? How had she? Her disgrace was his; her fears, his. Didn't she know that?

Something had cracked that night; some horror had come and it had leveled them. But this wasn't true distance; it was an invitation to closeness. A terrifying closeness that each was afraid of. They had to keep looking at each other, thought Julian, however awful the sounds of cracking, however scary the crashing of waters. Looking at each other.

That night they had come to each other, naked and vulnerable. That night they'd drowned together, drowned in pleasure and crazy pain. Blood and seed and sweat and everyone's tears. Everybody he loved was crying that night.

Lily, he thought, are you crying now? I am crying, thinking of you. We washed up on different shores, but we'll find each other. We're more alike than we've ever been, however far apart: drenched and laid low. We're slow, and we're frightened, and we're very tired, but we are going to find each other.

Peter said, "Julian, you mustn't cry like that."

He sat down on the bed, and took his brother's hand.

"If you do, I'll cry, too. And I haven't cried for years."

He wasn't really sure why he suddenly felt so sad.

"She's leaving Oxford, Julian. I guess I should tell you that."

"But she's coming back to finish her course, isn't she?"

"No, I don't think so."

"But Peter, why now? What's happened now?"

A part of Peter wanted Julian quit of her. To recoil from an involvement so exacting, so overwhelming. To laugh at it. Then they could be men of the world together, blades in tailored suits, laughing. Then he'd never lose his brother, or have to pray to be lost, himself, to an equal passion. Which he knew might never pass his way.

But a part of Peter, the better part, wanted love to rise above revulsion, fear and mockery. No one had ever made Julian feel the way Lily made him feel. This gave Peter a strange sweet feeling, as though certain once-loved notions of his, since degraded, defrauded, were not worthless after all. If Julian could not be laughed at now, raw as he was, he could never be laughed at. There was a sweetness in this hope. It was much sweeter than derision.

Peter wanted to poke at Julian now, to provoke him, to enable his heart to flex its unknown strengths. He wanted to see those unknown strengths, to learn from them. He felt like saying many things to Julian, true or untrue, just so long as they were provocative of feeling; he wanted to witness the force of lover's love. He felt like saying: she's dying; she's pregnant; she hates you; she forgot you. She's killed herself because you never wrote; she loves another man. She'll meet you on the sand, at dawn; she'll marry you tonight. She's right outside that door. Just open up that door.

"Tell me, Peter," said Julian. "I can see it's something big and horrible. I see it on your face. Please tell me."

"She's going back home. America."

He stopped again. She had said she wanted to tell Julian herself.

At the word "America," Julian lost heart for a moment, seeing Lily vanish into the vast continent, disappearing amongst skyscrapers and prairies, limitless heights and breadths. Now he'd never find her. Julian had never been outside of Europe.

"To her parents?" he said.

"Yes."

"Do you have the address?"

"Haven't a clue. But she's going home to her parents because she's, she's . . . "

He was going to tell; to hell with her. This was his brother. And Lily knew he could never keep a secret. Perhaps she knew he would tell. Perhaps she wanted him to tell.

"Well," he continued, fighting the urge to turn away, "it's the oldest reason in the world. After seven or eight weeks, there was no mistaking, I suppose, that she was, you know, pregnant and now she's off to have the baby. Couldn't very well have it here."

He looked at his brother. A smile was playing on Julian's face, which he covered self-consciously with a hand. Peter went on again.

"So I suppose you're better off without the public humiliation, eh? Wouldn't want her sobbing on your doorstep, would you?"

"I don't believe it," said Julian, softly.

His tone revealed that he did believe it, and was shaken. But there was no trace of horror in his voice. His hand fell from his mouth and he smiled a dazzling smile up at the ceiling. He remembered how he'd come that night. He remembered their words: what if? What if? It is a funny thing when the possible comes vividly and inescapably true.

"The most amazing thing," he said, his voice almost inaudible.

Julian began to feel happy, and even lucky. This meant something. Even if he slept, or felt a doubt, or if she did, the baby inside her was growing. There was no answer to that growing life. They couldn't tell it a thing; but it could teach them things there were no words for.

"You're frightened, aren't you?" he said to Peter.

"*I'm* frightened!? Aren't *you* frightened?"

"Oh God, yes. It's very nice. The fright. The thing I couldn't bear was not knowing. How could she tell you and not me?" Tears suddenly flooded his eyes and he blinked them away impatiently.

"I'm not really crying—I'm just, you know, Peter," he blinked again, tears flowing, "j-j-just overwhelmed.

"Something big like this just happens, like a mighty squall at sea and we ought to be able to—God, where *is* she? What's wrong with her?"

"She's too clever by half," Peter answered. "She thinks she knows everything, and she doesn't. I'm surprised by you, to tell you the truth. I feel a burst of brotherly respect. She's sold you short, if you want my opinion. Thinks she knows all the answers. Wants to run off now, and show her people what a pretty job she's done with the English in England. Got a baby to show for it, a baby all her own. I think she's got some idea of never seeing you again. Raise it in her image—raise you in her image, that sort of thing. It's a feeling I get about her. And I'm usually right in my hunches, you know.

"She's always been that way, full of notions and plans and plots. Always something cooking with her. Know what I mean?"

"Yes, sort of. Yes, I do. It's funny, it's sort of like your play, isn't it? No wonder she looked so stricken when I saw her in the interval. It was her look that made me run off to The King's Arms, Peter. She looked possessed by her own morbid thoughts. I felt I could never get near her, never penetrate that calcified misery."

"But you have, you see."

"Yes. Yes, I have." He sat motionless for a moment, letting this wisdom flood him. "Why does she never stop analyzing? I'm not letting her 'think' this one through, I'm not. It's pompous of her; it's cruel! And she's the one who'll suffer most from this this Oxbridge-clever thing!"

"Envy, envy," Peter chided, raising a long finger.

"No. I don't envy you constipated lot, if you must know. When I'm through with her," he said, filling his mind with fierce, pleasurable imaginings, "she won't have a thought left in her head."

"What a sweet thing to say, Julian!"

"Don't bother being sarcastic. It's far from sweet. I'm tired of her torments."

"Well, it really is quite true, what you say about our difficult Lily," said Peter, putting water on to boil again. "And it's too bad, because she exhausts herself making everything fit into its place. Does it come of studying literature, do you suppose, and having to write sensible, clear-headed essays about bits of beautiful gossamer? What a nice phrase. I shall use it in my next essay. Beautiful gossamer. Very nice.

"Well, that's her problem in a nutshell. Nothing does stay put, does it? You can't pin it down with your brain. I've always found it best to muddle through and see what turns up."

"Well, perhaps she doesn't feel safe enough to muddle through," said Julian.

"Oh, look," said Peter. "Danger's a cult for her. That's what I think. An old family habit."

"That's rotten. Stop it. I've shaken her up. I haven't made her feel safe. I want to, now. She deserves to feel safe."

"You deserve it too, Julian."

"Oh, I'm not worried."

"Aren't you supposed to be going to Bog-land or something?"

Shelagh Eveline Fanning, in her enthusiasm for Julian, had arranged for him to visit at the Abbey Theatre in Dublin, where his own father had trained and performed. If he liked them, and they him, perhaps he could begin training the following autumn.

"I'll go another time." But one of Julian's hands made snakes from his black hair, and his sky-eyes flickered dark.

"Don't get all impulsive and silly now. What does Archibald always say? Follow through, lad."

"And what about Lily?"

"Listen here, youngster, love has patience."

"Not when love is pregnant."

"Of course I know that, imbecile. I've kept gerbils, as you well know. Do talk to her. Tell her what's happened. That you might actually be able to have a calling, a *métier*, like everyone else in the world, and not merely drift from staircase to staircase here, looking up skirts, etc., etc."

"Tell her, and go to Dublin?" This cleared the air, and Julian, relaxing for the first time, lit up a Gauloise.

"Yes, rat. Get the girl, get the job, get everything I've ever wanted. Go on, you lucky bugger. And I'll tell you what. Tell her you've got some dough as well. Dad gave me a stash for my twenty-first which I haven't spent; I'll lend it to you. See if she doesn't react with a wee little smile."

Julian reacted with a broad, brilliant smile.

"You're not so bad, you old bender."

"Get dressed! Go! Run!"

Julian got dressed and ran over to Lily's college. Her enormous steamer trunk sat prominently in the lodge. It had a large white sticker stuck on the top. A New York address was written on this sticker with bold magic marker. Julian sat on the trunk and ground his fists into his eyes, pushing back the stinging tears.

"What's wrong, lad?" asked the porter.

"I'm looking for Lily Taub. Has she gone?"

"Let me think for a moment. The American girl?"

"Has she gone?"

"Yes, lad. Saw her go out about an hour ago."

Julian borrowed a pen and a scrap of paper from the lodge, and jotted quickly.

34

WHEN JULIAN GOT BACK to Gloucestershire that evening, he raced upstairs. He did not greet, but could visualize, Timmy in his special chair, eating "toad-in-the-hole," Helena picking listlessly at her small potatoes, and Archibald wiping gravy from satisfied lips. Julian wasn't hungry. His stomach was hard and flat, as though braced for challenge or the sharp relief of laughter. Having Lily's address had restored in him a feeling of power. He could reach her; he could move her. He had moved her: she was carrying his child.

He stood in front of the mirror, as he'd done all his life, and saw his power to capture and sway. His impending trip to Dublin enhanced this view: he would mesmerize them, both there, and, come springtime (as Caliban) in Oxford. The girl could run wherever she liked, he thought, but she was his. "I will people this world with Calibans!" he roared. The mirror reflected his cavernous mouth and strong teeth. He seemed to see, emerging, an appetite to reckon with: it came from his own gut.

"Hungry, darling?" His mother's voice, his enemy's voice, tickled up from downstairs. Hers was a young voice, eerily young, young enough to have a tremor of hope when it rose: "Darling?"

He wanted to answer: "I am never your darling," but realized the words would emerge with a passion that could only call her nearer. She did not call for him again.

But there she was, knocking very lightly on his door.

The witch, he thought.

"Come in," he said.

"Busy?" He stood up and started to pack some shirts into a bundle. As he moved, his mother's eyes followed him around worriedly, and he composed a letter to Lily: "Don't worry about Helena Kendall," it would say. "She died a very long time ago."

"Something wrong, darling?"

"What do you mean?"

"Are you going somewhere?"

He continued his imaginary letter: "She died a very long time ago, when she gave up my Dad."

"Why are you packing?"

"Going to see Dad," he said flippantly. "Popping over to see your ex."

"To France? Why, Julian, you were just there before Christmas! You keep flitting here, and there, and everywhere! How on earth are you ever going to amount to something?"

"Well, this time, actually, I'm flitting 'cross the water to Dublin-town. To freedom."

"You mean your father is now back in Ireland?"

"I'm going to the Abbey."

They both knew what he meant.

"How in heaven's name! Did he get you mixed up in that?"

It would be just like him, to grab at her heart from afar.

"He didn't."

"Who did?" She thought for a moment. "Is this that obese Fanning again?"

Helena did not appreciate Peter's interest in the Oxford acting clique; now it had infected his young brother.

"Well, as a matter of fact, you're right. She saw me wandering around Oxford and she got sort of intense about me. Said I looked like good old Dad. Thought I could let it out. Acting-wise. Without holding it back.

"Turned out I could! Poor Peter; he was so hurt. The one thing he wishes he could do, the one thing, and Fanning said—don't tell him this, Mum, promise—she said that she couldn't even believe we were brothers!"

To his surprise, Helena's eyes shone with delight.

"Well, you were special from the minute I saw you, I must confess," said his mother. "Different from Peter, as the bright yellow sun from the moon."

After a moment, she added, "You were the moon, darling; you were the cool, dark night with silver glowing through it."

She looked at him intently, and he met her eyes.

"The face of an angel, Julian, and always, always understanding, without anyone having to explain. I never worried about Peter; he was a bookworm, keen and sharp. But you, you," she found herself starting to cry, "by day you suffered; it was cruel; there was no place for you.

"But every night we used to talk; remember, darling? You had the soul of a confessor. Always absorbing, never judging, fading into darkness when you slept, so still and quiet. So still and quiet. Storing up your soul, I used to think." She sniffed, collecting herself. "I suppose it is something that she saw the specialness in you."

"And it's about time, too, Mum," said Julian, warmly. "Because I was never good at anything."

"Going along with your eyes. You were good at that. Listening, in that way that you had."

And even now, his face was following hers, responsive to every nuance.

"And you were loyal to the core."

"But Mum, that has nothing to do with real life. Men have to be good at things. They have to be agile, and clever, and fierce, oh, you know; it's so boring."

"And all I could ever do was make girls lie down."

Helena turned her face away, as though she herself had been one of those poor girls, now doomed to wander unclaimed.

"So I thank my lucky stars," he said, ignoring her, "that this has turned up. The Abbey Theatre is an amazing place. I want to act. I can do it, I think, and maybe do it very well."

"No, darling," she said, turning back with an efficient, matronly expression, "there are many things you can try when you're older, when you might have more stamina. Now look here. Of course you can go and have a look at those theatre people. I'd be the last one to stop you having fun."

Fun, he thought, and here I'm prepared to work hard for the first time in my life.

"Just a week," he said, "it's just preliminary. If I'm lucky, I'll be back there."

"Fine. But then you really ought to sit down and have a long talk with Archibald."

"All talks with Baldy are long," said Julian. This wouldn't be the first one, either. Archibald wanted him to go into a firm and work his way up. That was the road of the bald and bored and portly.

"You're lucky to have a step-father who, through sturdy, consistent effort, has lucrative connections to share. Things would be quite different if he were one of those artistes," she said primly. "We'd be living on mealy potatoes, for one thing."

Archibald looked like a potato, now that he thought about it.

"Can you imagine it?" said Julian. "Our Baldy as Prince Hal?"

Helena's lips parted in the beginnings of a smile, a little girl going along with a mischievous brother, hoping (despite herself) for the picaresque and prankish. Then she collected herself.

"No, my dear, I can't. But I can you, and it scares me. Actors play at being well-born, you see, wearing their fine clothes, and speaking in their fine accents, but they're not like us. They're just vagabonds, really. How on earth do they make a living? Just tell me that. Busking and begging, I should think, like raggle-taggle gypsies!"

"They work in a company, usually, like, like . . . " he was about to recall his rogue father again, who (as she very well knew) had travelled in a troupe across the Western world, but concluded, surprising himself, "a company like Archibald's. And they work hard, as well."

Fanning had told him that performers were like athletes of the soul, their work exhausting. And that first of all, there would be class after class of exercise: fencing, elocution, dialects, dance. The rhythms of body and breath, refined to a disciplined practice.

(Julian didn't know, but it did cross and linger through Helena's mind, that he had been conceived, in scorching love, during his father's provincial tour of *The Taming of the Shrew*.)

"Oh, really, they work hard like my husband Archibald."

"Yes, really. They give you a role, and you play it. Then they give you another, and another. You get up and go where they tell you to go."

Even now, at home with his dubious mother, he was starting to travel away.

"You eat, you drink, and sleep. You dream rich, dreamy dreams.

Everything you need is in your grasp: your mind and your body and heart and the page."

"And then you pack it all up in a trunk, I'd imagine, all wrinkled and mildewy. And I can't imagine they bathe too much, either, theatre people."

She looked at him, coolly breathing twin jets of smoke through his fine nostrils.

"Don't smoke those horrid French cigarettes, dear; I'm beginning to think it can't be healthy."

He took the last drag through to the butt; she watched his breath make orange fire and lazy, blue smoke.

"I suppose that huge, odd woman thought you quite dashing, then."

"Fanning? Well, I guess. But she did make me audition, Mum. I had to read pages and pages of Shakespeare, Wilde and Shaw. I had to read Stoppard, Mum! It's not as if it all went to her head or anything. She didn't rave non-stop. She said my work showed 'brilliance, mixed with nonsense and mistake.'"

"All right, look," she said, after a moment, "I'll tell you what. Why don't you try an easy summer job at Archibald's firm, and if it doesn't suit you straight down the line, then you can do all the play-acting you like."

"What you don't understand," he said, beginning to lose patience, "is that this is Peter's final year. I'm not even supposed to be hanging around Oxford. I'm supposed to have my own life. I've finally found something. Shelagh doesn't get ecstatic every day!"

"I should hope not. It would be exhausting to watch."

Helena caught a glimpse of herself in the mirror, sitting next to a young man, dashing enough to be a film star, and realized that she would be cast only as his mother.

"And what's more, what's more," she burst out, "I don't want a son who roams. I don't want a wild horse!"

She thought of Timothy, growing sturdy and strong; he was already cantering on his pony with inbred authority. She saw the man this child would become, but she could not see this man in Julian; she saw many men. He could grow into one thing, and then another, and then another, of indeterminate nature. "I don't want this artifice," she said, thinking of enchanted forests, wishes three, of kisses that grant kingdoms, and spare lives. She thought of mythical creatures she couldn't name. Half man, half boy; half child, half lover. And oddly, painfully, she thought of the Jew, familiar and strange. She thought of Lily.

"I don't!" she found herself shrilly shrieking. "Not this job! Not that girl!"

Julian grabbed her shoulders, hard, and she shuddered and went still.

"I love the girl," he said, slowly letting go of his mother. "And I will love her to Ireland and all the way back."

"Oh, honestly. This is getting silly. We've discussed this, haven't we?"

She rose shakily, her blouse slightly disheveled.

"Every time you want to upset me, you utter her name as though she were the good Madonna. Archibald!" she shouted.

Her movements, her voice, were almost vulgar.

"Yes dear?"

"It's Timmy's bedtime, isn't it? Come up immediately."

"Just coming," Archibald said after a moment.

"I think we've worn each other out," said Helena to her son.

"I love Lily, mother, and I'll love her wherever I go," he responded evenly.

Archibald stood in the doorway, Timothy in his arms. Helena shot her husband a glance, and he responded sympathetically: two parents standing witness to a child's persistent fever. He took her by the hand, and the three of them left Julian behind.

"What story did you hear tonight, sweetie?" Helena asked Timothy.

Aloft in his father's arms, he met her face to face. They walked into the child's room.

"Sleeping Beauty!" he stated emphatically. "Everyone asleep for many years! Like statues outta stone! Until a prince!"

"Very nice, darling," said Helena, stroking his soft big head, as Archibald laid him down on the narrow cot. Julian, who had quietly followed the procession, stared at the three of them with an odd, thrilling terror: they made a family of stone, of which he was no longer part.

"And the prince woke everyone up?" coaxed Archibald.

"Yes!" Timothy kicked his feet happily; the father, who had leaned over, got knocked in the gut.

"You're not a goat," said his mother, grabbing his feet. But she could hardly hold his goat-feet back.

"Lily is carrying my child," Julian suddenly said. "She's gone, for now, but I'll fetch her back."

"And very happy then!" squealed Timothy, still thinking of the tale.

His feet rested, and he popped his thumb into his mouth for a muse, like a man with a good cigar.

"Everyone awake," he added, wide-eyed and contentedly observing the commotion.

"A child," said Helena, stunned. "Do you mean to say yours?"

"Perhaps you'd better talk about this elsewhere," said Archibald sternly. But no one moved. Timothy, sensing the lull, resumed kicking until Archibald, with uncharacteristic crossness, called out:

"And if a little boy kicks like that, he will not be carried, but will march all the way, like a man!"

Timothy shrieked in horror. Helena fled from the room.

"What a chaos tonight," she thought, covering her eyes, and shuddering untameably.

Julian, returning to his room, was rattled too. But when he had finished packing his case for Dublin, he put his thoughts on paper, addressing the letter to Lily's American home.

35

THAT NIGHT, Lily had a dream about going home.

The airport was a hard and lonely place. People were running back and forth, or waiting like dull animals. All destinations seemed diagnoses. Billeted, terse "Arrivals" and "Departures." Equally melancholy in this sterile place, this traveler's ward, this waiting room for wandering spirits. No one from England could help her now. They couldn't say, "how riotously funny!" They couldn't say, "how unspeakably sad." She followed the sign for "Departures," surrounded by Jews. She walked through the tunnel and into the womb of the great plane, which was sealed shut. But all through the voyage, sweet air (and not poison) came through the vents, and she reached New York unafraid. There she saw her father at the Passover table. He wore a holiday skullcap of satiny-white, with gold arabesque, and she smelled spring in the air, earthy and strong and eternal. Where am I? Jerusalem? And Julian was there, suddenly, and said: "Yes, Lily. Welcome home."

No one could see Julian. He was inside her, filling her with light, and she glowed like a temple on an ancient hill.

She tried to explain: I met a righteous gentile, she began, smiling, almost laughing, with pleasure. If she laughed too hard, she'd float away to heaven. She stopped herself by thinking, they're my parents. I must explain until they understand. But the words came out wrong. I met a beast-man, they heard her say. I met a Caliban. A lover-boy, a noble-savage.

They seemed furious. As grim and as frightening as ghosts. She squeezed her eyes tight to get rid of them. Baby's bones sprouted from Polish pastures. A harvest of skull and crossbones. Voyaging, pillaged. The moon shone on an orange earth that reeled like lava; corpses sprouted like potatoes. She rocked her head from side to side, trying to shake ugliness. But there was Timothy (or was it her own dead half-brother?), rocking with her, stuck to her heart like a rotting barnacle.

And the baby was bawling, freezing and wet.

What am I carrying here, she wondered.

Is this the Messiah?

She screamed out:

"Tell the Christians I'm tired of watching. Tell the Jews I'm tired of waiting."

36

A WEEK HAD GONE BY, and the steamer trunk still sat laden in the lodge. Lily could not decide what to do with herself. True, if she waited until the last minute, her trunk would arrive weeks later than she, but clothing was the last thing on her mind. Right now, mid-afternoon, she was wearing a bathrobe over nothing. When her parents phoned her that evening one on each extension asking what she planned to do, she answered vaguely.

Over the phone, she heard her mother mention that she had received a postcard from Ireland. "Signed J.A.," she said. "Do you know who it is? The card just says three words: 'Rest, perturbed spirit.' Isn't that peculiar," said Gretta. "Yes it is," said Lily, knowing that the words came from Shakespeare, and from Julian.

"Who do you know in Ireland?" Josef said. "A wonderful person," said Lily. "I'll tell you all about it sometime." She intended to tell them everything, when she herself knew it all.

"Would you please send me the card, right away?"

"To where? To your college? Fine," they answered lovingly. "But don't you want to come home, anyway? Don't forget Passover," they said. "It's always on my mind," she said. "The way the Jews travelled over the water to freedom. The way they travelled, over raging water. To safety," she said.

"So travel the Atlantic, then," said Gretta. "I've got all your favorite foods. "*Kol Dichfin,*" added Josef, which meant, "all the needy." On Passover, all the needy people may come and partake. "That's me, all right," agreed Lily, wearily. "*Kol Dichfin,*" her father repeated, teasing, "our starving waif is welcome at the table."

Actually, she felt nauseated more often than not. When she hung up the phone, she resumed reading *Romeo and Juliet.* At least those two were both Italian, she reasoned glumly.

A loud rap on the door, which she recognized.

"Open up instantaneously, cow."

Cow! It seems they were friends again in earnest. She opened the door and he preceded her into the room.

"So you're still here. You can't hide from me. And where's my drink already?"

Peter seemed to think that adding "already" to a sentence made him sound completely Jewish.

"I'm just getting it, already," she said.

She obediently took her vodka down from the bookshelf.

"All right, then. I'm parched. No! not one of those silly little glasses. Give me that bottle," he said sternly. "I've brought my own straw."

"Where'd you find that?" English straws were rarities, especially the plastic, striped and bendable model that Peter was wielding.

"Oh, Mum got it for me on her annual jaunt to Harrods. Got me a box of 'em, in fact, in lots of colors" he said, sucking vodka, "and I love her for that, if nothing else."

"Ever see the kind with flavor in them?" asked Lily. "Chocolate, strawberry, you know, you kind of jiggle them in the milk, and it turns—"

"Oh, Christ, I forgot!"

He dug under his jacket for a bottle in a bag. Lily thought for a moment that he was replenishing her vodka supply, which, try as he would for a lifetime, he could never do. She grabbed the bag and pulled out a quart of milk.

"It's Gold Top," said Peter proudly, "the premium dug-juice. Loaded with cream."

"I don't like milk."

"Give it here, don't whine."

He took the bottle from her and put in one of his straws.

"I gave you a blue one for boy," he said, shoving the bottle at her. "Now drink." She drank. "I want a fine, healthy nephew."

"Or niece," she added.

"Mm hmm," he said, calm again, imbibing his own.

"Or niece. A fine town, by the way. *Nice.*" he looked up. "I like homonyms."

"Like 'hymn' and 'him," she agreed. There was a comfortable pause, and they both sat musing.

"Nice isn't far from Cannes," said Peter, breaking the silence.

"I know."

"So I like it," he said, "because my Dad has chosen to live there."

"I know."

"A chic *émigré*. Like you."

She sort of went for the sound of that.

"Could I trade with you for a sec?" she gestured at the booze, feeling suddenly festive.

Peter jumped up and started waving his long arms in the air like windmills.

"All right, all my suspicions are confirmed! You have no right to carry that baby without constant supervision! Do you know, for example, what alcohol can do?"

"Don't lecture me; it'll live longer if I don't commit suicide."

"Yes, with a head like a pin, and bright magenta bow wrapped around three very long hairs. If it's a boy, it will have no goolies, and if it's a girl, it will have no teats, not one, and no man will love her!"

"Oh, I guess I won't drink, then."

"And don't go committing suicide, either. What do you want to do that for?"

"Because I don't know what else to do?" she ventured shakily. "I thought I was going home, but I don't know, and Julian just wrote to me from Dublin "

"That's good. Many spelling errors?"

"What? Oh, leave him alone, I don't know;" she said, fretting the belt of her bathrobe, "he mailed it to my parents." She thought a moment. "I suppose you told him everything."

"Well, I told him quite a bit. He took it manfully, my dearie. And I also told my mother. And here is what Mum has written:"

"No, Peter. Spare me."

"I didn't spare him, and I'm not sparing you. I wish to God someone wouldn't spare me. My life's a bore.

"Now pay attention."

He took a note from his pocket and began reading:

"Peter, you must tell Lily how very welcome she'd be at our home."

"You meddler! I can't go there!"

"Shhh." He went on, "how very welcome she'd be at our home. We understand the embarrassment of her situation"

"They don't like me," she said, "it's in the subtext. 'Embarrassment,' for instance—"

"Shut up! Let me finish."

"and we'd all very much like to be a family to her. Soon, she'll be showing, and people with their many questions, will be unkind. Here, we have space, and shelter, and heaps of love to go around."

Folding the letter away, he found Lily thinking, with a tentative, childlike look in her face.

"Still subtext-hunting, eh?"

"I'm not sure," said Lily. "Space, and shelter. Heaps of love to go around." The words sounded true from her lips. "A family to me. It would be nice," she sighed. "I'm very tired."

"I'll be there too, you know, and Julian's coming back any day."

She was very pale. "I think I have to vomit soon."

"Go do it now. Go on."

She ran out of the room and came back a moment later.

"False alarm," she said, "my body's gone crazy!"

"To think you were planning to fly for hours and hours. I won't have it. Do seat belts stretch so wide, I wonder, anyway? I suppose that's why you haven't bothered to get dressed, you slag."

"Oh, come on, I hardly show!"

"That's what you say, Mum," he said. "Amazing. Suits you. Mum. Now you and my mother have the same name."

"Oh, yeah. We're bosom pals now."

"You're both incredibly bull-headed, that's for certain. So essentially, you're twins. And what have I always, always told you?"

"Loads of things."

"Blood's thicker," said Peter, draining the bottle with a noisy slurp. "And now you're in the bloody thick of it."

37

L
ILY ARRIVED, a few days later, with Peter and her trunk. It
was early evening, mid-March. The countryside was peaceful and still, and the moon shone softly in the sky. The cold
was not as fierce as she remembered.

Helena Kendall opened the door and took Peter in her arms.
"Welcome home, darling," she said. Peter wasn't used to this at all.
Then Helena let go and did the same to Lily.

"Welcome home, darling."

"Hello, Mr. and Mrs. Kendall," Lily said, though Helena's collar
muffled her voice.

Helena wasn't letting go, and her grip, surprisingly strong, sent
a charge through Lily's body, head to toe. Archibald peered over his
half-glasses with a faintly sad expression, as though he wanted a hug
like that too (and never had received one).

"Good to see you, young lady," he said.

"Hullo, Lil," said Timothy, a bit cavalierly.

He'd been instructed to be "especially nice" to her. When Lily
was at last able to turn around, she saw the familiar yellow hair and
round, round eyes, staring up at hers.

"Hi there, Tim," she answered.

She noticed that he'd shot up over the past few months; his
body was beginning to acquire Helena's (and Peter's) rangy look.

"Have you had a good winter?"

"In-like-a-lion-and-out-like-a-lamb," he said, in one breath.

"That's March, darling, that's close, and when in March does winter end precisely?"

Lily nearly fielded the father's question, but it (along with Archibald's patient stare) was meant for the little boy.

"Dunno."

"Yes you do, Timothy, on the twenty-first. And how many seasons?"

"Twenty-first," his son said, still echoing the first point.

"Where's your cat?" asked Lily.

"My Whiskers?" Timothy looked touchingly grateful for the interruption of his catechism. "My Whiskers having his tea in the kitchen. I had mine. I ate fish-fingers."

He held up three fingers to show how many he'd had.

"You had four, darling, not three," Archibald chided. "Three plus one makes four."

"Three or four, as long as you enjoyed them."

Lily felt wistful. How could she ever have feared the little child?

"You two must be famished," said Helena, interpreting Lily's wistful look as hunger for fish fingers.

"No, we ate on the train," said Peter, grabbing Lily by the hand.

"Come on, I'll show you your room."

"I know where it is," she whispered, embarrassed. "Shouldn't we stay down here and be sociable for a while?"

"You can come back down a little later," he said, pulling her up the stairs. "Let's get you settled first."

He opened the door on the clean little room with its freshly made bed, and they sat down next to each other.

"I'm terrified," she said.

"I know. Your eyes are all bulgy."

"Shouldn't Julian be back already?"

"I guess it's going really well over there for him. He must be seeing a lot of people and everything. It's not as though he even knows you're in England. He'll be so happy to find you here."

"So convenient," she muttered.

Peter put his hand reassuringly on hers. She looked up at him in surprise, but did not feel repulsed.

"God, I love you, Peter. You know that, don't you?"

He grew bright red.

"Hey, Peter. So you don't know everything, after all."

She brought his hand to her lips and kissed it. His hot cheeks and delicate, heron-like features, so unlike Julian's brashly carved ones, made her feel he was a shy Victorian (a Victorian spinster, maybe). Her only impulse was to make Peter feel treasured, beautiful.

"What are you doing?"

She slowly put his hand down.

"I think the hormones of Julian Junior are making you cross over to the berserk side."

"Maybe so."

She looked down sadly at her lap. Her hair shone softly in the light. He reached out his hand, tentatively, and stroked it, patiently, the way her father did when she was a girl. It was a light touch, undemanding. Her hair rustled softly, like a wing, by her ear.

"You silly," he said, "with your naughty thoughts and deeds. Look, we've had a long day."

He got up and put her suitcase on the bed.

"Unpack, and let poor Peter go to sleep."

"Wait. Don't go. What'll I do? I'm wide awake.

"Do I just go downstairs and sit by the fire as though nothing happened?"

"Yes. Do just that and they will, too. They're the best actors in the family, those two."

"All you English are pretty good at that. Acting like it's just another day when your house has burnt down and you're running into the street, naked."

"Grace under pressure makes heroes, my darling." He paused by the door and added, sternly: "You must get some."

38

L ILY DUTIFULLY CREPT DOWNSTAIRS and sat by the fire, as though nothing had happened. Whisk was sprawled along the hearth like a tiger-skin, but otherwise, she was entirely alone. The grandfather clock ticked audibly as she flicked through a dog-eared *Horse and Hound*, and after a few minutes of this, she decided to get up and browse through the larder. Bread and jam would hit the spot right now, she thought.

As she neared the kitchen, she heard her name mentioned, but only faintly, as though in a ghostly dream. The retort of a deeper voice, urgent, almost manic, brought her back to reality:

"Why on earth she doesn't . . . ."

"Not Julian's problem, surely, and he certainly doesn't want . . ."

"And supposing that we . . ."

"Is she eligible for the National Health?"

"Now, Helena, even if . . . it would hardly be seemly for us to . . ."

For you to what? Lily fought to hear better, so hard that she shook. She took a small step closer. Suddenly, they went silent. After a moment (during which the grandfather clock tick-tocked enough to drive her mad), Helena and Archibald resumed their conversation.

"The point I'm making, Archibald, is that my son is simply not mature enough to handle this sort of responsibility, and if we cannot persuade the girl to . . . "

"I will persuade her," said Archibald, his voice rising.

"But on the other, hand, if we took the child and raised it as though ... "

"I will persuade her, Helena, because I will not have disgrace brought upon my house. There would be a blot on Timothy's name, and such a blot I will not stand for!"

"Sweetheart, we could adopt the child, legally."

There was silence.

"You know I can't have any more children. Wouldn't it be nice for Timothy to have a playmate? Peter was so happy, dear, so happy when his little brother Julian was born. Just think, it might be a little dark haired boy like him. Think how darling they'd look together: Timothy growing taller by the day, with his fair hair, and a plump, dark toddler adoring him." She paused for a moment. "I could go away for a while, you know, and we could even say that it was mine. Perhaps someplace warm, the Riviera or something, and you could meet me on weekends, or maybe take some time off from work."

"How very foolish you sound!"

"Archibald," she said, sadly, "will you never be foolish for me?"

Lily shook so much that she made a small noise, like the squeak of a mouse, but luckily, they didn't seem to hear it. She began to back away, slowly, from the kitchen. When she had reached a safe distance, she flew up the stairs to her room and sat, panting on the bed until her tears finally came. She sobbed aloud, half-hoping to be heard by Peter, but he did not return to her room.

"Why crying?"

Timothy had heard, and he had softly padded in.

"Because I'm sad."

"Why sad?"

"Because I'm terrified."

"Why terrified?"

If this game got nowhere, perhaps it was because she was not being frank enough. So she told him something true which he might somehow understand:

"I'm terrified, Timmy, because nobody cares about me, nobody can help me, and I'm, I'm very sick, you see," she held her stomach. "I have a tummy ache that's grows bigger and bigger by the day."

Timothy understood. "Because you greedy?" He remembered! She nodded vigorously.

"Yes, Timmy. I am greedy, and now I'm very, very hurt, right here."

He put out his hand, and she let him touch her belly. He stood there with his small hand on her stomach, thinking.

"I go get Mum-Daddy," he said, "Mum-Daddy always help me."

"No, don't. This is a very funny tummy-ache. Only Julian can help me, you see, and he isn't here yet."

She started crying again.

He stared at her in wonder.

"Why crying again?"

"Because it hurts again and again."

"Ohhh." Timothy, though pensive and fairly sympathetic, yawned widely.

"Should I put you to bed now?"

"I not tired." He paused. "O.K."

He gave her his hand and they walked to his cot. He crawled into bed and she covered him.

"Ju-ian come soon?"

As she foraged for an answer, she noticed that the little boy was dreaming.

39

JULIAN DID, IN FACT, COME SOON, but when he arrived and learned that Lily was not beyond the seas but in his house, he felt a sudden panic. Awkwardness gripped him. The first few words he spoke to her were impolite.

"Whose idea is this?"

That didn't seem to call for an answer, so Lily turned angrily away. He let her go. A few minutes later, wrapped warm in a jacket, she burst out the door to take a long walk by herself. He let her go. He saw her when she came back, flushed, pretty, and touchable. A little warm roundness under her zippered red anorak, a touch of frost in her hair, and eyes that would not settle.

And later, descending the stairs with Peter's arm around her, she followed the family into the dining room.

Julian walked out of the house, coatless, and tramped down the road.

"Where are you going?" Peter called out.

He kept walking, fast, feeling thrown out of his own house. He couldn't stand his mother's insinuating face, acting as though she had a little secret. Peter was even worse. Who did they think they were, bossing him around and shoving her at him like that?

The Abbey had been fantastic; had they even asked him about it? No. They had all had to stare at him, smiling a little, seeing how he'd "react" to the sight of the girl he'd got pregnant. Well, good luck to them all.

They had loved him in Dublin, as a matter of fact. Some had remembered his father; he'd had kid-glove treatment. And acting had given him a sense of freedom: a sense of scope and sway that everything in that nosey little regime denied.

"Could do with a pint of bitter," he thought, heading for the local.

He felt manly as he entered, taking in the rumble of voices and tinkle of glass, the smell of good beer and the smoke. He stood at the bar and asked for his pint, eying the pies as well. He was suddenly ravenous.

"I'll have chicken and mushroom," he said, "and a Scotch egg."

Over in the corner, he noticed his neighbor, Nicola, sitting with a few of her friends.

"Home for Easter?" he called out, jovially.

"Julian."

Nicola was shy and lovely. She stood up and walked over to the bar.

"Come and join us?"

He hadn't seen her since New Year's Eve, when they'd danced. Now he remembered her blond hair, flying, losing the scented violet ribbon that had held it together.

"It's been a long time," she said, remembering too. "How've you been?"

Nicola cared about him. Look at that. Right away she wondered how he'd been.

"I'm great," said Julian. "Couldn't be better."

"Your mother keeps telling me to come round," said Nicola, blushing, "but I never have the nerve."

"Does she?"

His mood sank minutely.

"Yeah."

"Well, I haven't been 'round much myself." He paused dramatically. "Been 'round Oxford, of course, and I've just come back from Dublin, in fact."

Nicola's eyes widened gratifyingly. He felt like a man of the world, a traveler. When the pupils enlarge, a girl's wanting it, he thought.

"Have you? Oh, Julian, how exciting!"

"Yeah," he said casually. "Been looking into acting, you know; if I feel like doing it, I probably can."

"Oh, Julian, what was it like?"

"It's really exciting, actually. All these really, really intense people, you know, in bursts, and then they stop, and they seem normal, even dull, in a way, and yet—"

Nicola was fetching, but as he spoke he began to feel an age old loneliness. His story, in sharing it with to her, was beginning to lose its flavor.

"And yet they're not," he concluded.

"Not what?" asked Nicola earnestly.

Her pupils were so wide, her eyes looked black.

"Normal. Or dull."

"Oh. Uh huh." His order of food came hot to the counter. "Sure you don't want to join us?"

"Who's 'us'?"

He peered over to the corner where three other girls were giggling. She waved happily to them.

"There's Caroline, Sue and Jackie. You know Jackie, don't you, from school?"

Yes, in fact he did. She was the one with the malicious giggle, whose lifetime goal it was to work in a "very flash office."

"Carrie and Sue are in nursing school with me. Oh, wait, Jackie's coming over to the bar."

Jackie stood there with Nicola and Julian as he ate his pie and Scotch egg. She seemed to be working up her courage to say something.

"Want some beer?" he asked.

"No thanks."

She tapped her crimson nails on the brass railing.

He drank his bitter, and waited.

"How've you been?" was what she came up with.

"You've changed a lot since school; you look quite chic now. Say, those boots are dead cool."

"Yeah, thanks." Jackie's lids were coated with a shiny blue cream, which clumped here and there in a fold. Her lashes were blue, too.

Nicola said, "Julian's been to Dublin, to an acting academy. Tell her about the actors, Julian."

"Well," he said, "they're all ever such a lot of fun, but. . . ." He felt his face get tired of holding whatever expression it was straining to hold.

"But what?" said Jackie. "I've heard they're all on the odd side."

She took Julian's glass from his hand and drank a long swig.

"God, that's awful," she said.

"Look, I'm sorry, I have to go."

"I'll walk you home, if you like."

This was Nicola, at whom Jackie glared.

"No, really, I've got to go."

He began walking out by himself, not quite knowing where he was headed. Jackie came scampering, breathless, after.

"Coming along then, are you," he said, walking faster and faster. "What a treat."

"Sure. I fancy you like crazy."

She ran alongside, having a grand time. Her bright blue eyes were ferocious.

After a few minutes, she thought to ask, "Where are we going?"

He didn't answer.

"God, you look like a murderer," she added, impressed.

Grabbing her plump arm he marched her, fast, down the lane, and over into the wood. After a few minutes he saw it: there, in a clearing, was the tree stump he'd lain on with Lily

"Lie down," he said.

He could not believe how fast she did so.

"Isn't this a terrific spot?"

"Oh, yeah; it's fab!" she nodded, scared, excited.

"Cold?"

"Just a bit. It's O.K."

"Want me to cover you?"

"Have you got a blanket?"

"With my body, I mean?"

She did not answer, but stretched herself out, like a sacrificial victim, and lowered her lids.

Julian lay down on her, but did not move.

"What's the matter?" said the girl, what was the name? Jackie. "What's the matter?"

A deep, hysterical sound came out of his gut.

"What are you doing, laughing? Huh? What's the matter with you!"

She tried to move his heavy body.

"You've always been off," she spat out, shoving him off her. He fell to the earth, heavy boots and all. She stood over Julian, screeching.

"You've always been off your head; you're just pathetic!"

She ran and ran away from Julian, toward lighted windows. He remained in the darkness, alone, on the ground.

40

AFTER SUPPER, Lily sat with Peter in front of the fire and wept in his arms.

"Why doesn't he want me?" she said.

Peter honestly didn't know. She looked into his eyes, her lashes bright with tears.

"It's over, then," she said. "I'll go home and have an abortion. That's what they all want, anyway."

She didn't tell him what she'd heard Helena and Archibald talking about. It didn't seem to make much difference, anyway.

"We could never have made it. It was silly to dream about it happening. It's just that that I can't b-bear the thought of killing something that was made of him and me, because- -"

"I understand."

"Because I love him, even—"

"Even now."

"Yes, Peter."

"Would you—"

"I can't do it all myself," she interrupted. "I'm not strong enough."

"Would you consider letting me help you, Lily?"

"How could you help me?"

"I could, you know, help you raise the baby. I've got quite a lot of money saved up, and I'm fairly sure I'll get a good job next year, so—"

She was slowly shaking her head.

"No?" he said. "You don't want that?"

"I'm finding it hard to think about, that's all. We're talking as though, as though Julian were dead or something."

"I'm sorry."

She took his face into her hands and kissed him. His lips were thin and dry. She kissed him again, as though that would make his lips blossom, full and moist with love.

"Mmmm," he said politely, "that's good." There was no desire in him.

She began crying.

"You're such a good person, you know that, Peter?"

"Oh, yeah, I know. Crème de la creamy."

"Because of you, I drink my milk every day."

"It's doing you good," he said, "you're getting huge dugs like dear old Sabina."

Lily looked down.

"You know, you're right," she said, smiling. "My baby won't starve."

They sat quietly, in sympathy, and night ticked on.

When Julian came home that night, he raced upstairs to Lily's room, and whispered her name fiercely. "Lily! Lily!"

Timothy, half-awake, answered, "Fix tummy now!"

But Lily was not in her room. And Peter, Julian discovered, was not in his, either. Slowly going back downstairs, Julian saw a horrifying tableau: his brother, older and cleverer, cozily slumbering with Lily in his arms.

After a moment, he trudged to his room and looking in the mirror, found nothing. No one. Just a fop, with the sad look in his eyes of a chronically lonely child. The Abbey was a dream, a delusion. They had responded favorably to him, but it was all vanity, foolery. Their encouragement had tricked him; he'd tricked them back. A show of bravado. Soon they'd see through him, and he'd be off to work for Archibald, or someone like Archibald. He had no talent, really; he'd never had anything but luck. And luck could not be counted on. Good luck had brought Lily to him; bad luck was washing her away.

Peter was down there, stepping into his life as though he, Julian, were a ghost. Taking his lover away from him, as though he were nothing.

Julian came back downstairs and stood by his brother and Lily.

"Give me back my life," he said, so quietly that only Lily heard him.

She woke up from a bad dream, and saw her lover standing in the room.

"Would you come upstairs with me?"

They went upstairs into her room.

"I don't know what to say to you," she said, looking away.

"Lily," Julian hesitated for a moment, and then the words rushed out like a waterfall. "I know only one thing, and that is that I love you. I was hiding from you, and my punishment was an immense emptiness. I used to think you were born on my doorstep. Now I'm willing to travel to you. If I'm a coward, I'm a brave one now. You can easily, easily, break my heart.

"On the way back from Dublin, the train had an interesting bunch of people on it, including an extremely polite Nigerian gentleman who was talking to a Dutch woman about his family. She in turn was talking about what an excellent standard of living there is in Amsterdam. I don't care where I live, Lily, as long I'm with you. I'll speak any language. I'll pray to your God. Lily, these things don't matter.

"A lady sat opposite with a big baby on her knee. The baby seemed to be very precariously balanced on the knee so that I thought every corner of the track would bring calamity. But no. While Mummy read *The Daily Mirror*, the big baby amused himself pulling faces at all the delighted fellow train riders. He stuck to that knee, as though by some supernatural glue force. What a thing this love we speak of is!

"There is slavery in love too. So we must be careful not to overwork the chains. Please don't harden your heart. You have a part of my soul. Not for a minute have I feared your custody. I have been careful with my own precious charge. You are inside me, and I am tender.

"I'm glad there is a baby growing in you. I've been reading Deuteronomy, Lily. 'Countless as the stars,' eh? Brilliant as the stars, anyway.

"And now there is one more."

Julian had never said so much at once, and for once, Lily couldn't speak.

"Does your tummy really hurt you, darling?" he asked. He had wanted to call her darling, but doing so made him blush. They both started laughing. It would take some practice.

"No, it's fine."

He sat down beside her and touched her on her stomach, where it rounded.

"Hello, in there," he said, bending his head toward their child. Lily closed her eyes and stroked his hair.

Some minutes wafted by, into their past, to be remembered. Time was slow again, and luxurious, because they were together.

"How was Dublin?" she said.

Julian told her about Dublin. It had gone well for him at the Abbey.

"First of all," he said, enjoying it for the first time, "it turns out that Fanning's reference means a hell of a lot, because she hasn't pushed anyone for years and years."

"I knew you were special," said Lily, calmly.

"And they loved my audition pieces, too," he went on, "and one of them said—I told them I was going to do Caliban in Oxford next term, you know, and he said—he wanted to be there 'to see history made.' Can you imagine that being said to me?"

"You can do anything. Look what you did to me."

"Look what you do to me. Look at my face. Do you know what they saw, Lily? Do you know what they saw? They saw a man in love, moonstruck and desperate and off my head!"

"I'm here," she laughed. For the first time in two months, she was happy. "It feels like you're going to die when you're not sure, doesn't it?"

"Don't worry about that, because I won't let you die. I'll take care of you forever."

"Well, well, well," she smiled, leaning back against the bedpost.

"Just wait. You'll see."

He noticed a picture of her parents on her night table. So that's who they were. Lily turned around and saw them through his eyes. Gretta's face seemed to be cracking slightly, showing the sadness below. She was craning her neck, as though for crucial information; her eyes were alert and her smile, strained. Josef was more genial. He had a face so full of ancient innocence that she wondered, as she would about a sick child, "Must he, too, die?" She couldn't stand to think about the death of either of them. Surely, after all they'd been through, couldn't God spare them the final blow of annihilation?

"It's a nice photo," said Julian gently. For a moment, she thought suspiciously of Julian's own photographs of the retarded teenagers on their outing. Was he being condescending? Were her parents, too, sad "specimens?"

"There is something about film, isn't there?" said Julian, not seeing her mood darken. "Maybe I'll do a film, in time, as well. You never know. A lot of actors do. We all want to live forever, I guess."

"Yes. We do all want to live forever. And some people deserve to. After all the effort to smother their small flame, they should never be snuffed out. They—they should be revived, and—"

"Lily—what's wrong?"

"These old people, these are my parents, and if you love me you have to love them, too." She had planted their photo there, in the Kendall house, out of loyalty. Still, she heard her voice came out more apologetic than defiant. What did she have to apologize for? The fact that she was born of mortal stock, not stone, not celluloid?

"They are my past, and I am their future."

"What are you saying?"

"What do you think?" she shouted, facing him as though he personified every obstacle to Jewish survival. "These are my parents! My people! The Jews are not going to die out on my watch!"

"Lily, I love them for giving you to me. What is it? What's troubling you?"

"I don't know, I don't know. I miss them."

He took the photograph in his hands and searched their faces. "They were very brave to let you travel, after all they've been through."

"I never thought about it that way. They showed me more love than I ever believed possible. But how did I repay them? By leaving them."

"You haven't left them, and you won't. They were very generous, to trust you to the world. I will repay that trust."

"How, exactly?" Lily couldn't help smiling at the simple way Julian saw things.

"I will love you like family, Lily. And I will always honor them, for giving you to me."

"That's nice. But how?"

Julian stood up. He took the photo in his hands and spoke to it: "We will raise the baby Jewish. I'd be proud to."

Lily was moved, but (being Jewish) a part of her mind remained skeptical. It had to ask questions and get answers before it could settle into solace.

"What do you know about being Jewish?"

"I know you—complicated, curious, insatiable you. And I want to know them. I'll stand among you. It's a start."

41

An Island in the Center of the World, 1977

ALIBAN WAS HIDDEN IN THE LEAVES of a great, old tree, but when the cue came, he dove into the water, then rose onto the land, shaking off droplets into the first three rows of the audience. His skin was covered with green, and brown; Lily was thrilled to hardly recognize him. And his voice was different, loud and coarse, and defiant with innocence. When Julian bellowed, "I cried to dream again!" he pounded his own face with frustration, and Lily cried for him. His face, when he cried, seemed to be crying out and away a lifetime of frustration.

During intermission, under the wooden bleachers, he smothered her with kisses, and she became, like him, covered with water, and green and brown. His eyes, up close, looked paler for being ringed with black, and, with one hand on Lily's shoulder, he nervously searched the milling audience. He fixed on a man with a highly animated expression on his face.

"That's the one from the Abbey, with Shelagh. See?" He hoisted her up.

"Yeah. Shelagh's winking at you. She must love the performance."

"Oh, yeah, she saw the dress rehearsal, so I'm not that nervous about my—Oh, God, that's my father," he said suddenly. "He's really come."

"Peter will be so glad!" said Lily. But she knew that he had come for Julian, and for her.

"Can you believe he actually came all the way to England?"

"It's not that far."

"It's worlds away. He hasn't been here for years!"

"What should we do? Go over?"

"No. Look. Peter sees him, too." Peter was edging through the crowd toward his father, waving gawkily. Dressed as Prospero, he looked stiff and uncomfortable. The father, dressed in an old tweedy jacket, gave him a hearty slap on the back and they shook hands with a single muscular jerk, like men.

"We'll see him later," said Julian. "When Caliban fades back into the night."

"I'm scared," she said softly. "He looks so much like you."

"Who? Caliban?"

"No. Your father. I see why your mother never got over it."

42

THE LIGHTS FADED, and the audience slowly drifted away. Even their murmurs were gone, and the warm June night was thick with silence. Trailing behind, the last to leave, Lily and Julian walked to the River Isis. Each boarded a small punt. The oarsmen drew them on, down the river, and did not turn to see a young woman, dressed in white (a costume donation from the OUDS clan), with flowers wound in her hair, and the young man, also in white. The river wound, round and round, through the shadowy medieval town.

In a third little boat, just ahead of them, sat Lily's parents. Their boat traveled the waters, which whispered in the dark of sorrows, forgiveness, and hope, reaching an area illumined only by a circle of candles. And there, around the circle, were Julian's father, and Peter, and Shelagh Eveline Fanning, and even Mrs. Dancer, glowing in the warmth of the flame.

Josef and Gretta Taub disembarked first and were warmly embraced. As their daughter's boat arrived, they reached out their hands to help her step onto the shore. Lily embraced her parents, kissing each one on their soft, old cheeks. Slowly, she released them into the circle of candlelight. Julian came last, walked over to her at the center, where they joined hands.

When the woman and the man stepped into this center, flowers rained from every tree, and small bells tinkled. There were actors up in the boughs, to send them on their way. Then, an old, silk prayer shawl, trailing long white threads from every corner, was spread out and held over their heads. It was a marriage canopy as Prospero would have made it, King of Magic that he was. Held by human hands, the shawl vibrated with the frailty, and bravery, of love.

Julian took Lily's hand in his and gripping it tightly, said,

Be not afeard: the isle is full of noises
Sounds and sweet airs, that give delight,
And hurt not.
Sometimes, a thousand twangling instruments
Will hum about mine ears;
And sometimes voices,
That, if I then had wak'd after long sleep
Will make me sleep again: and then, in dreaming
The clouds me thought would open and show riches
Ready to drop upon me; that when I wak'd
I cried to dream again.

And looking all around her, and above her, Lily, responding, cried:

"Oh, brave new world, that has such people in it!"

To which sentiment, Peter pealed, "Amen to *that*!" causing everyone to laugh, including the young female Rabbi from Headington.

Minutes later, after reciting the requisite vows, Lily and Julian were declared "husband and wife." Julian then stomped on a glass, shattering it into shards. He had learned that every joy brings sorrow, and every sorrow, joy, that temples are devastated and mourned, but also rebuilt.

So, after the stomp, there was a happy commotion. The isle was full of noises, sounds, sweet airs, and "Mazel Tovs," that give delight, and fade, after long revels, into stillness.

43

I N TIME, Lily would give birth to a little girl, breathing companionably upon her mother's breast. A funny little thing: blue eyes streaming under pale lids, wet black thatch sticking out in all directions.

Brilliant as a star.

This would happen in Ireland, where Julian began his career. In time, they would travel throughout, and beyond, the dwindling British Kingdom. They would travel to London (where Peter lectured), and Edinburgh, to Tel Aviv and New York City and all the way to beneficent Miami, where Lily's parents would spend their happiest years. Lily, observing, remembering, would write about it all: how a man leaves his family and cleaves to his wife. How a world is made, destroyed, and restored when the lion and the lamb reconcile. She would write about how grandparents hold babies and sense the divine, a taste, at last, of what we all call eternal.

But for now, Lily had no thoughts beyond the wedding circles on her hand and on her husband's. They were as golden as the light that traveled across water and land, rising to greet them as they woke up in each other's arms.

Acknowledgements

This book was written roughly twenty-five years ago, and would not have seen the light of the 21st century day were it not for the loving ministrations of my editor and publisher, Ellie McGrath, founder of McWitty Press. I think it is no small coincidence that the imprint's title contains not only the word "witty," but also a near-rhyme to McVitie, manufacturer of England's finest "digestive" biscuits: Ellie is that wise and that nurturing. I would also like to thank Stephanie Sosnow, Debra Berman, Lynn Schwartz and Susan Weinstein, all of them wonderful people and loyal friends. Abby Kagan and Jenny Carrow lent me their visionary skills, and I am grateful to them for giving such a beautiful face to my ideas. My husband Paul was a wonderful support during all this midwifery, as were my children, Emma, Gabriel and Phoebe. Lastly, I am grateful to my late parents, Simon and Gita Taitz, for their enduring love and support for my every venture, romantic or practical.

꽃

About the Author

Sonia Taitz is an essayist, playwright, and graduate of Yale Law School and Oxford University, where she received an M.Phil in Literature and was awarded the Lord Bullock Prize for Fiction. Author of *Mothering Heights* (William Morrow and Berkley), her work has appeared in *The New York Times*, *O: the Oprah Magazine*, *People*, *The New York Observer*, and many other publications. Her plays have been performed in Oxford, New York, and Washington, D.C.

In The King's Arms is her first novel.

Reader's Guide

1. What do you think is meant by the title of *In the King's Arms*? What sort of kings are there in the book, and what types of power do they have? Is their power real in all cases?

2. How do you explain Lily's desire to leave her parents and her homogeneous, Jewish world? Is it heroic bravery, or an act of betrayal? Why does she feel a need to move away? Is her move to Europe more shocking than if she had, say, gone to Canada or California?

3. This book is set in the 1970s, with flashbacks to the war-torn 1940s. To what extent is Lily living in her parent's time? Are her fixations and fears relevant today? Do we still live in a world in which so much depends on where one comes from and what God one worships?

4. Why do Lily and Julian choose each other? Will she be happy with him? Will she feel safe, in the way that Archibald does, in the world they will create together? Will Julian?

5. The book contains flashbacks into the horrors of the Holocaust. Does this background explain the insularity of Lily's parents? Is this insular-

ity vital to the preservation of their Jewish culture? In other words, do cultures need to be protected from both prejudice and assimilation?

6. Do you think Lily's parents will ultimately be able to embrace Julian as their son-in-law? Will Lily's journey open their hearts and/or help heal their wounds? How will Lily's daughter see the world?

7. Are Julian's mother and step-father as insular as Lily's? What motivates their strong feelings? What has happened to their vision of Great Britain in more modern times? What has happened to the idea of nationalism?

8. Do you think love will conquer all, as the final chapter suggests? Does this book resolve the problems faced by Romeo and Juliet? What would have to happen in the world so that people like Lily and Julian can truly build a life together?

9. *In the King's Arms* is not just a story about love but about reconciliation. In what ways does Lily show her desire to reconcile Gentiles and Jews? What drives this desire?

10. Do we still face the old cultural vendettas with which previous generations struggled? What forms do they currently take? Do you wish, as Lily sometimes does, for a common "communion"?

An Interview with Sonia Taitz

Q: What made you decide to write this book?

I was compelled to write this book by an insistent idealism. I truly believe that, as Anne Frank so famously said, "people are basically good." The beauty of love, its openness and trust, convinced me that I could write a story in which walls of distance, hatred and prejudice could fall down between loving people.

Q: To what extent does this novel reflect your own upbringing?

My parents were refugees, Lithuanian-Jewish survivors of the Holocaust in Europe. As their daughter, I was taught from a very young age that Jews were permanent targets of a vast, undying hatred, and that I must be vigilant. Slowly, I developed a different sense of the world, my own sense of possibilities. Of course, expansiveness was easy for me—I grew up in America in a prosperous and idealistic time. Women, people of color, worshippers of different religions—all these so-called minorities were absorbed and accepted as equals in our culture. I wanted to step out and show my parents (and myself) that this new world was "basically good," and that Jews were no longer the sacrificial lamb of the world, as they saw it.

Q: How did you "show" them this?

They themselves came to the same conclusion as they grew older, perhaps aided by my academic and professional success, both in

America and in Europe. My father was especially proud when I got into Yale Law School; it convinced him that in America, an immigrant's child could do anything. When I went to Oxford, he was even more bowled over. His own schooling in Europe had ended abruptly, as had my mother's. In his case, his father had been killed by the Cossacks when he was small, and he had to begin working soon after; in my mother's case, a career as a concert pianist was aborted when the Nazis came into Lithuania.

Q: Did you practice law?

Yes, for a time. It was my father's wish—in urging me to go to Law School—that I "save the world," but what I mostly did in the early years was help major corporations fight enormous cases that dragged on forever. More recently, I returned to the law as a pro bono *advocate for foster children as well as victims of sexual and domestic abuse.*

Q: When did you become a writer?

I'd always written, starting from high school. At Oxford, I wrote fiction and plays. I wrote this book during my time as a corporate litigator. I got an agent immediately, and made thrilling plans for a life as an "artist." My agent found many interested editors; several asked to meet me. One, a grande dame *with her own imprint, spoke to me in her office for hours as we drank tea from porcelain cups. Regrettably, she decided against publishing* In the King's Arms *(and that year published an English writer who is now world-famous!). Next, a senior editor, from a prestigious, small house, invited me in to discuss his changes for the book. If I made them, he said, he would make me "a literary event," and a certain critic from* The Washington Post *would review me on the front page. So I went home, made the changes and. . . .*

Q: They didn't publish the book?

That kind of thing is quite common, I found. The senior editor loved the changes I made, but his publisher decided against the novel because he had just acquired something similar—another book that took place in Oxford.

Q: What year was that?

Oh, about 1986 or so.

Q: You mean, 25 years ago?

Yes.

Q: Does that kind of time frame make you want to give up on writing?

No. I got a book called Mothering Heights *published by the estimable William Morrow, and enjoyed a heady ride (media blitz, paperback, foreign rights), which is unusual for us writers. A struggle is far more typical. So it's a good thing that I am a dogged idealist, as struggle is what I faced despite the relative success of that first book. My new memoir, rejected by dozens of publishers (despite my having the best agent in the world), is coming out next year. Like the Jews, I like to beat the odds by surviving. And in the end, art, like any true love, is always worth the effort.*

Q: What attracted you to write a book about two young people from different cultures?

I am always interested in polarities and how to reconcile them. I am also a product of two cultures: orthodox Jewish, born and bred in a Yiddish-speaking immigrant's ghetto; and American, happy, bold and optimistic. I see the world through two lenses, each with a different view. It's dizzying, at times, but the perspective is inspiring.

Q: Do you think the young lovers can conquer their cultural and religious differences?

My husband is a passionate convert to Judaism and past Board Member of our lively synagogue; so, yes.

Q: Do you think this reconciliation is important for the world at large?

My response comes perilously close to John Lennon's "Imagine," but I do envision a world in which ancient hatreds and rivalries can be soothed by bonds of love. Not necessarily romantic love, as in this novel, but open-heartedness. Perspective. Compassion.

Q: How autobiographical is the book?

As I've noted, my husband comes from a non-Jewish household. We have three beautiful children, all "brilliant as the stars." As I recount in my forthcoming memoir, my father, at his deathbed, said: "Thank you for bringing these people [my husband and his family] into my life."

Q: This book takes place several decades ago; how is it still relevant today?

Unfortunately, hatred and race prejudice are still all around us. I believe that words are equally powerful, and that is one reason that I will always be a passionate writer and reader.

Q: What are your next projects?

I hope to see my memoir in print next year, and I am working on a new novel.